SECOND SHOT WITH #76

PIPER RAYNE

This book is a work of fiction. Names, characters, places and incidents either are products of the author's imagination or are used fictitiously. Any resemblance to actual events or locales or persons, living or dead, is entirely coincidental.

© 2022 by Piper Rayne

All rights reserved, including the right to reproduce this book or portions thereof in any form whatsoever.

Cover Design: Okay Creations

1st Line Editor: Joy Editing

2nd Line Editor: My Brother's Editor

Diversity Editor: Renita McKinney

Proofreader: My Brother's Editor

About Second Shot with #76

My mom always said you don't get a second shot at making a first impression. I've remembered that my entire career. Especially since I'm one of the few black men who play professional hockey.

I'm calculated and respectful in the way I speak to my coaches, the owners, and the media. I've never taken a risk… until her.

I could blame it on the fact that for once I pushed away the pressure of my career for the ocean waves, the sand, and good times with my new teammates. But those are excuses because the minute I saw her at the airport, something lit up inside me and the best week of my life was spent with her in my bed.

After our week in paradise, we said goodbye, exchanged phone numbers and both assumed that unless one of us was flying through the other's city on the opposite side of the country, our vacation fling was over.

Then one night after practice I see her. She's here. In my city. Telling me she moved here for a job. If that's not fate tell me what is.

I've never wanted a second shot more than I do this time, but she's determined to leave what we were on the island we left behind.

Second Shot with #76

CHAPTER 1

"It's your business."

Cory

Most would say I'm living the dream. The veterans on my team, the Florida Fury, tell me to live it up, that it doesn't last forever. And I have to say, being a professional hockey player, even as a rookie, isn't bad. Sure, I'm not seeing my jersey on every kid's back like our first-line center, Aiden Drake, but I get to play my favorite sport for a living.

The cameras, the interviews, the strangers asking for selfies aren't really my thing anyway. I've always been shy in that respect, since my dad put a lot of pressure on me growing up about how I represented myself. He's always told me that you don't get a second chance to reinvent yourself. Oh sure, people say you do, but everyone still remembers that thing you did.

My phone rings in the center console of the new sports car I bought when I was drafted down here. Seeing my dad's name on the screen sours the burrito I just ate. The man stalks me more than the puck bunnies after a game. But I can't ignore him.

The Bluetooth kicks in as I answer the call. "Hey, Dad."

"When will you be able to keep your dick in your pants?"

"Franklin!" my mom hollers in the background.

"One of these days, you're gonna get someone pregnant and you'll have a baby mama who wants that paycheck of yours, not your dick."

"Franklin!"

I sigh and flick on my turn signal. I don't know where he finds this stuff. "What did you see?"

"I search your name every morning and a new article always pops up."

"And?" I wave to get this conversation moving even if he can't see me.

"You were in the ocean with some woman. It's pretty clear from the pictures what you two are doing, even if it is fuzzy."

I blow out a breath, remembering Ande for a moment before I wonder why the hell some outlet would be reporting about us now. Ande and I had a vacation fling while I was at my teammate, Ford Jacobs's, destination wedding months ago. Hell, Ande was my start to sleeping with random women. Of course, I hooked up some in college, but that was nothing like what it is in the pros. My teammates are right.

"Dad, I'm young. I'm not gonna apologize for enjoying myself at my teammate's wedding. Any other guy in his twenties is out there—"

"And how many guys in their twenties are living their dream of playing professional hockey?" He cuts me off with his typical tone of authority.

"Not a lot, but that doesn't mean—"

"I know what it's like. I do. But let me remind you that you have a responsibility to your people, to represent us in a positive light."

I blow out a breath. "I'm just having fun."

"Well, if the fact that you're a role model for so many

young Black boys out there isn't motivation enough, how about your mom crying after church the other day?"

My arms straighten and I force my back into the driver's seat, annoyed he's pulling a guilt trip on me. "Why was Mom crying?"

"Because of these articles. We're a small town and you're not representing us well."

"Why do I have to represent you? I'm just being myself."

"It's an honor to represent your hometown. And if being yourself is having relations with a woman in the ocean with hundreds of witnesses, then you're not the son I know and raised."

I groan and wonder if telling my dad about Ande is even worth it. She wasn't some random, though there isn't a future there. Hell, what do I have to lose?

"She was different, okay?"

"If she was so different, then why all the women after her... oh." The light bulb goes off. "She's the on—"

Now it's my turn to cut off my dad. "I'm not saying that. I'm saying I was interested in her, but she lives thousands of miles away and I reached out a few times but got nothing in return."

"So you decided to go on pussy patrol?"

"Franklin!" Mom shouts in the background.

"You know better. That's not how these things fix themselves."

"I know, but I'm only young once."

That's the line Tweetie told me last season when we were in Chicago and I was on the fence about staying at the hotel with Warner instead of going clubbing with the other guys. Tweetie was adamant that I shouldn't sit in a hotel room. That's what guys like Drake and Jacobs did. Men who had found the love of their lives. I'm not sure how he envisions Tedi, his longtime girlfriend, but I will say he didn't even dance with another woman while we were there. At least when I saw him.

"That sounds like some bullshit a teammate said to you."

How can he possibly know that? "Maybe I have to experience different women to know what I want?"

He groans. "Your mother is the only woman I've ever been with and somehow I knew she was the one for me."

"I guess you're better than me." I check over my shoulder and change lanes, then shift gears and press my foot down on the gas.

"I'm warning you to cut this shit out. I'm not being hard on you because I'm mad about these articles. I called because it's upsetting your mother and you know whose side I'm always gonna be on when it comes to your mother and someone else."

"Even your own son?"

"Yes. Unapologetically yes. But if you keep this up, Cory, the talk is gonna be about what you're doing off ice and not what you're doing on it. Got it? Is that what you wanna be known for? How many women are in your bed on game nights rather than how many goals you scored?"

"It's not like I'm getting a ton of ice time," I grumble, pulling into the parking lot of the Florida Fury arena.

"We talked about this. You gotta pay your dues. Your time is coming. Especially now that you guys have Langley. Aiden Drake is an exceptional center, but your time will come, son."

"When all my good years are over?" I'm whining because I'm pissed about Ande now that my dad has brought her up. I thought we had a real connection and for her to just ghost me after we returned home from the island pisses me off.

"Don't."

"Don't what?" I ask, parking my car and letting it idle while I watch my teammates walk into the arena.

"Feel sorry for yourself. You made the right choice."

Mr. Gerhardt asked me point blank whether I'd be okay sitting on a lower line for the first year or two when he considered drafting me. Otherwise, the Sharks were willing to take me and I'd be a starter, but that team is crumbling. That's how the Fury got Langley—they needed the money from his salary off their books. I didn't want to be a star who never won a Cup. I want to be on a strong team that wins the Cup and, if we're lucky, multiple years in a row.

"I know I did."

"And as for the girl, it's best to put your personal life aside for right now. Train, eat healthy, and make sure you're one-hundred-percent ready when your number is called up."

I nod although my dad can't see me. "Okay."

"I'm only hard on you because you've got something special that doesn't come around often. How many Black men are in the league right now?"

"I get it."

"Then show it."

"Yes, sir. Listen, I gotta go. Practice is gonna start soon." My finger hovers over the end call button.

"We love you," he says.

"We miss you!" my mom yells.

"Clear your schedule up for dinner when you play St. Louis? Your mom and I want to take you out."

"Done."

"Good. Love you, son."

"I love you."

We hang up and I sit there for a moment, thinking

about what my dad said. He's always right. Sleeping around isn't earning me anything except a reputation I don't want.

A bang on my window startles me, and I turn to find Warner Langley standing there. "Do you want to be late?"

I open my door and we file inside since all our gear is already in our lockers.

"You're coming tonight to the barbeque, right? After practice."

"I don't have a side dish yet."

Warner is having a get-together tonight after we're done here, and we're all supposed to bring a side dish.

"Imogen and the girls are shopping after practice. You can go with them. Text me when you guys are on your way back."

"What's going on?" I ask since he's being vague.

"Nothing. I just have a surprise for her." He pats me on the back. "Thanks for helping out."

Warner speeds up to walk alongside Ford, and the two of them whisper to one another for a minute.

It's still weird seeing them be close. Up until a couple months ago, Ford was set on making Warner's life here miserable because of some shit that went down between Warner and Ford's sister, Imogen, when they were teens.

In the locker room, I sit on the bench and suit up for practice. But I quickly get distracted and pick up my phone, wanting to know what article my dad read. I wonder if it holds some sign that I missed when it came to Ande. I've never had an instant connection with a woman like I did when Ande sat next to me on the bus that would take us from the airport to the resort. It was almost as if I knew her in another life or some shit. Jesus, I gotta get a grip. I'm losing my fucking mind over a woman I knew for less than seven days. A woman who wouldn't even return my phone call. Several of them, in fact.

It doesn't take long to find the article, and I think it's popping up again now because there's a new comment on the thread that's tickled the algorithms. I read the comment and my hand clenches tighter around the phone. It's from a woman who says I slept with her two weeks ago in Los Angeles and never called afterward. That I made her feel like Cinderella, treating her like a princess until midnight when I demanded she leave my room.

Such bullshit. First of all, I never have sex in my room because I share one with Warner when we're on the road and he'd be pissed. I always go to the woman's place... *Fuck, listen to yourself, Freeman.*

As if the universe is trying to drill home what a douchebag I've been, a new text message arrives.

York: *I'm due to come to your area of the country in a week or so. No specifics yet. I know we only hook up in Denver, but I thought it might be fun somewhere different. ;)*

I met York at a bar the first time we played Colorado and she keeps tabs on me, so it's easy to hook up with her every time I go through town. And unlike the woman in the comments, York doesn't care that there are no strings attached.

Me: *If you want tickets let me know.*

York: *You know I don't care about hockey. Just be sure to reserve time with you.*

Me: *You got it.*

York: *I'll keep you in the loop. In the meantime...*

A picture pops up of her tits. Damn.

"You're really taking this whole manwhore role to heart, eh?" Kane Burrows, the Florida Fury goalie, sits next to me and looks over at my phone.

"I don't ask." I click the button on the side of my phone to turn off the screen.

He's quick to raise his hand and shake his head. "It's your business."

He puts on his equipment. Kane is older and probably in his last couple of years in the league, but I've developed a sort of mentorship with him. He's been in the league so long, there isn't much he hasn't experienced.

"I just mean I don't ask for them."

He nods, then shrugs. "But you accept them."

"What am I supposed to do?"

He chuckles and adjusts his pads. "You're not supposed to do anything. We've all handled it differently over the years. Take Tweetie for instance, who was a lot like you his first few years and, hell, many years after. Jacobs wasn't exactly keeping it in his pants. Some players are just more discreet. Like Drake would get pussy but rarely did anyone know about it."

"And you?"

He chuckles again and pushes his hand through his chin-length hair. "I've been through my phases, but I learned a long time ago that I want my name on people's lips because of my ability in front of the net, not because of how many baby mamas I have or how much I pay in child support. Or worse, how I imploded my family because I couldn't keep my dick in my pants."

I lace up my skates, thinking of what Kane said. I know I

need to figure out my own path in this league, carve out a place for myself. Let's face it, right now, my personal life is way more interesting than my professional life. I'm getting a shit ton more sex than I am ice time. I guess if I want to change that, I'd better spend more time practicing on the ice than fucking in the sheets.

Step one is to forget I ever met Ande Evans. The whole reason I've been sleeping with so many women is to try to erase her from my mind. If I can forget her, maybe I stand a chance of getting my shit together.

CHAPTER 2

Ande

*H*ONK!

"Jesus, Ande." Trevor holds the car door handle as if I'm going to get us into an accident and he's considering bailing.

"What? I'm still getting used to these roads." I pull into the grocery store lot.

"The roads are different in Florida compared to Salt Lake City?" Trevor's arched eyebrows lift to his hairline.

"Shut up." I playfully smack him in the chest.

"It's not really cool to tell your boss to shut up." He opens his door before I have the car fully parked because he has to be dramatic in most things.

"Then don't ask me to pick you up and help you cook dinner for your date." I climb out of my car. It's new, but nothing fancy. The beater my parents gave me in high school never would've made it here when I moved.

"I think we have the perfect work relationship." He swings his arm around my shoulders and kisses my temple. "Plus, you owe me. I gave Janice the hard account, and you got the easy one last week."

I punch him in the stomach, and he pretends I actually hurt him.

I'm not sure what I would've done if Trevor hadn't

hired me and taken me under his wing. Leaving my two best friends, Sophie and Brit, left me feeling a little lost. After the fling I had with Cory in the tropics, I thought we had a connection, so I looked him up now that we were practically neighbors, but what I found online told me the only connection we'd had was that we were both horny. Finding all sorts of stuff online about his playboy ways told me he wasn't pining away for me. Sure, he'd messaged me a few times when he was coming through Salt Lake City, but I wasn't interested in being his booty call again. He didn't know it, but I was already in the same town as him.

"No preferential treatment," I say.

"If you can't throw your new bestie a bone, then what's the advantage of being the boss?" He grabs a cart and propels himself forward.

I take a small basket to grab a few things for my dinner for one. "Let's pick up the pace. I have things to do tonight."

"Like what? Watching your pathetic DVR shows? What is it tonight? Bravo housewives or *Married at First Sight*?" He picks up a grape and tosses it in his mouth, then his eyes widen as though he's thought of something. "You know what? You should go on that show. *Married at First Sight*."

"Yeah, no." I peruse the fruit. "It's crazy how good your produce is here."

"I wouldn't know the difference, I grew up here." He takes another grape and throws it up in the air, but it hits the corner of his mouth and rolls across the floor.

"Okay, let's focus. Do you know what kind of food your date likes?"

He pushes the cart forward. "Nope. It's a blind date."

"Trevor, you don't invite a blind date to your house."

He shrugs. "It's fine."

"You have to woo him. What if he's the one? Or worse, a serial killer?"

Trevor laughs and pushes the cart like an adolescent who can't control himself. He's going to hit some grandma's heels, and she's going to smack him in the head with her shelled purse.

"I'm going to check out the meat." He winks and disappears.

I look over the prepared salad bags, hoping to find one that isn't starting to go bad already, shaking my head at Trevor. I love that guy.

"Ande?"

My hand stills on a bag of salad.

That voice.

The one I heard in interviews when I stalked him on social media. The same one I still have saved as voice mails on my phone.

I circle around and it's him. Cory.

When I first moved here, I used to picture running into him, but figured the chances of that happening were slim. A bachelor's life is very different than mine. Especially when the bachelor is a professional hockey player.

"Cory," I say, trying to act as surprised as he looks to find me in Florida.

He leans forward and I do too, but we draw back right before going back in for an awkward hug where his lips touch my cheek. I swallow down the sigh that wants to escape my lips.

"What are you doing here?" He runs a hand over the stubble on his face.

"Funny thing. Right after I got back from my trip, I was offered a job here. So…"

His smile grows. "You live here now?"

"I do."

For a moment, I forget everything else. The booty calls he made to me when the Fury was playing Salt Lake City, the fan site with pictures of him with other women, how hurt I was when I realized that I was just a vacation fling no matter what he'd led me to believe. I'd thought Cory was different, but he was the same as them all.

"That's great." He looks around and frowns at whatever he sees behind me right before the sound of oranges toppling from a display has me turning around.

"We thought that was you," Imogen says and comes over.

One at a time, all the hockey players' girlfriends reveal themselves from behind the orange display. Tedi, Saige, and Paisley wave before hugging me as though we're long-lost friends. I met them on vacation and they were nice, but I don't know them well.

"You should come to Imogen's. She dates Warner Langley now," Tedi says.

I laugh. "I saw."

How could anyone not? The man poses for every damn paparazzi photo with Imogen tucked under his arm. He might as well wear a T-shirt that says, "My heart belongs to Imogen Jacobs." As you can see, I'm not the least bit jealous.

"Their billboard, you mean. Yeah, he can just stop now." Tedi puts her finger in her mouth.

Imogen blushes.

"Well, I'd love to, but..." I stop, not sure what else to say.

Cory groans.

"You know what? We have to go. I forgot Warner wants sausage. Big, thick sausage," Imogen says.

"Nice." I smile.

"Did you hear yourself?" Tedi pushes Imogen forward,

then turns to us. "We'll meet you at the cashier. Hope to see you there."

Once they're gone, Cory and I stand there awkwardly. I don't know what to say. I've both dreaded and looked forward to this moment.

"I should go." I thumb in the direction I was headed. "It was great seeing you."

He shoves his hands in his pockets. "Hey, do you have a new number?"

And there it is. I need to decide if I should cut ties altogether with Cory. But damn, half a year as a pro hockey player and his body is transforming in ways that make me drool. And that's while he's fully clothed. I can't imagine him naked… okay, yeah, I can visualize.

"Hey, love." Trevor approaches us. "Got the meat." He holds up a package of some type of meat with a huge smile and puts it in his cart. "Oh, I don't need salad. I don't much care to eat anything green."

Trevor doesn't seem to even notice Cory at first, but Cory is busy looking him up and down as though he's sizing up the competition.

"Oh, who's our friend?" Trevor asks, then a strangled cry comes out of his mouth. "No! Oh my god. Are you trying to pick up Ande right now?"

I scoff and turn to him. He covers his mouth with his palm.

I slide my arm through my friend's and Trevor looks at the movement in confusion. "Cory, this is my boyfriend, Trevor. Trevor, do you know Cory—"

"Freeman! Jet from the Florida Fury. I just figured it out." Trevor sticks out his hand.

I hope he'll go with the white lie I just told. It was a split-second decision, and it just seems easiest to end the possibility of something with Cory.

"That would be me. So, you two are dating, huh?" Cory shakes Trevor's hand, his eyes on me.

"Yep," I answer, instilling my voice with confidence.

"How the hell do you two know one another?" Trevor stares at me, waiting for the answer.

I never told Trevor, or anyone else, about Cory because I think deep down, I knew that it probably was more meaningful for me than it was for him.

"We met at a resort last summer. In the off-season," Cory says.

"Tell me, Cory, if someone was going to make you dinner, what would you want them to cook?" Trevor asks.

Before I know it, the three of us are walking the aisles of the grocery store. Cory is actually telling Trevor what to cook and I'm annoyed. Trevor is an intelligent guy. I'm pretty sure he can put two and two together—like my awkwardness toward Cory and the fact he keeps trying to start a conversation with me while Trevor bulldozes him with questions.

Before I realize it, we're at the checkout with all the hockey girlfriends.

"I can't believe you know someone who plays for the Fury, Ande. Why didn't you ever tell me?" Trevor asks.

Tedi's eyebrows crinkle in confusion.

"Girls, this is my boyfriend, Trevor. Trevor, these are all the girlfriends of—" I don't get a chance to finish before Trevor jumps in.

"Imogen Jacobs, you date Warner Langley," Trevor says, pointing at her with a big smile.

"That's like the free bingo marker. Try another one of us," Tedi says.

He shrugs. "I just saw the Instagram post."

"You and everyone else." Tedi rolls her eyes.

"Hey now, there's no reason to be so snippy about him loving me. Don't we want the best for one another?"

Paisley puts her hand on Imogen's shoulder. "Of course, sweetie."

We get through the round of introductions and Trevor seems thrilled by the prospect of meeting all the hockey players at a barbeque this afternoon, though I'm trying to give him a look that says I want to do anything but. Imogen gives me her address and tells us we can follow them to the house.

After we say goodbye and I get in the driver's seat, I put the keys in the ignition and look squarely at Trevor. "We're not going. If I happen to see any of them at some point in the future, I'll just say we got lost."

"We are not skipping a party with the Florida Fury." Trevor turns to me with wide eyes as if I'm crazy. "Plus, what's up with the lie about me being your boyfriend? I'm clearly gay."

I shrug. "You can do straight."

"Just because I know hockey does not make me seem heterosexual." He crosses his arms and stares out the front window.

He's right. Now I feel like an ass.

"Listen, I hooked up with Cory at that resort. I was there with my friends to try to forget about my last boyfriend, who'd cheated on me. Met Cory, we hooked up, and I thought there might be the potential for more. Turns out I was just a puck bunny who got lucky because I got him to myself for a week."

"That man still has something for you. He couldn't stop staring."

A blush heats my cheeks. I shake my head. "He probably just wants to get laid."

"Whatever you say, but you owe me. We're going to a private party at Warner Langley's place."

I put the car in drive, and he reads me the directions, shooting question after question at me about Cory. There isn't much to tell, other than his persona doesn't match what's coming out of his mouth most of the time. He told me I was some rare attraction he doesn't usually indulge in. In reality, I'm just the girl he wanted on that trip, and I made it easy for him to have me. But silly me believed him.

"I can't wait!" Trevor claps like a toddler. "We should've brought wine. What did you buy?"

"Salad."

"All I got is the meat, but that should do. They're all big muscular hockey gods, right?"

"What about your date?" I ask and glance at him.

"Just canceled. What are the chances that a blind date will be better eye candy than a roomful of professional athletes?"

I pull down a long driveway and park behind a bunch of other vehicles. Trevor is out of the car in a shot. Before he can grab the meat, Saige rushes over to us as Imogen walks up to the door of the luxury beach house.

"Come on, Warner planned a surprise engagement," she says in a hushed voice.

"Shut up!" Trevor says and turns to me with incredulous excitement on his face.

Saige smiles and nods. "Yep, so we have to go around the back of the house to get there before Imogen."

Trevor sprints around the house. By the time I catch up to him, we're directed to stand in a line that Imogen is walking down the middle of toward Warner, who is waiting for her at the end. God, I'm so uncomfortable with us being here when we don't belong.

"May I remind you, you're only here because of me?" I whisper into Trevor's ear.

"And I plan on being the best pretend boyfriend ever!"

Warner grins at Imogen when she reaches him and starts in on his speech.

Feeling someone's gaze on me, I look over and see Cory's watching. I offer a smile and slide my hand down Trevor's arm to hold his hand. He squeezes to tell me he's here, but I probably picked the worst guy to try to sell as my boyfriend. I know all this man candy will be a distraction for Trevor. Hell, it's a distraction for me.

CHAPTER 3

"Welcome to the club."
—Ande

Cory

I step back to double-check the address on the business card Trevor gave me yesterday and find that it matches the building I'm standing in front of.

This is probably a mistake. I keep reminding myself I should be glad Ande is happy with Trevor. But something seemed off with them last night and I want this gut feeling to go away. Some part of me needs to make sure she's safe, that she's not involved with the same type of guy who'd left her heartbroken when I first met her.

I open the door of the office building and find a row of mailboxes on the wall and stairs in front of me, along with a small hallway leading to the back door. Since they're in Suite 205, I take the flight of stairs then open their office door, peeking inside.

I'm surprised when there's a receptionist and a line of offices along one wall, cubicles on the other side. I'm thankful I'm getting to live my dream because I cannot imagine having to work in an office all day. I think I'd feel like an animal in a cage.

"Can I help you?" the young woman at the receptionist desk asks, and I walk over.

"I'm here to see Ande Evans."

Trevor walks out of what I think might be the break

room with a donut in his mouth. He pulls the donut from his mouth with his hand. "Cory?"

"Hey, Trevor." I walk past the receptionist and shake his hand.

"What brings you here?" He looks around for Ande, I assume.

"I wanted to give you and Ande some tickets to the game tomorrow night." I pull them out of my pocket.

He has no idea how hard I had to fight for actual tickets I didn't have to text or leave at will call. Who knew they made it so difficult now? I have every stub of every game I've ever been to. There's sentimental value in an actual ticket.

"Seriously?" He looks at the tickets and his eyes bulge when he sees where they're sitting. "First row?"

I nod. I'm considering making Drake an offer to feign an injury to get some more ice time while Ande is there. "Only the best."

He tilts his head. "How do you know Ande again?"

We were able to dodge that question last night and I need to keep dodging it because he'll see my motives for exactly what they are—to get his girl to fall for me again.

But only if she's not happy in her current relationship, I have to remind myself.

"Is she here?" I ask, dodging the question—again.

He tucks the tickets in his back pocket and bites his donut, leaving a spray of icing sugar all over the front of his shirt. "Right this way."

I follow Trevor to the corner cubicle that looks out over the road I just parked on.

"Ande, look who surprised us," Trevor says.

She swivels around and bolts up from her chair. "Cory!"

Her cubicle is small, so she practically runs into me.

Trevor finishes eating his donut while I grab her arms to keep her steady.

"Sorry, I'm a little light headed. I've been staring at this logo for an hour." She steps away from me but not closer to Trevor, staying in a neutral territory.

"Then let me take the two of you to lunch."

"Oh... I'm on deadl—"

"You should go, Ande." Trevor waves her away.

"I have to get this package finished by the end of the week and the client has to sign off on the logo first. There's no way I have time." She looks at me. "Sorry."

"Hey, no problem. Maybe after the game tomorrow, we can all go to Carmelo's. It's where—"

"You guys all hang out after! We know of it." Trevor gleams.

"I don't know of it," Ande says. "What game?" She looks at Trevor, who wipes the sugar off his hands.

"I brought you and Trevor tickets to the game tomorrow night."

She eyes Trevor.

"Front row, babe!" His excitement is clear. The guy must really love hockey.

"Oh, thank you," she says to me.

"Now I insist the two of you go to lunch." Trevor gives her a meaningful look I can't decipher, but I decide I'm starting to like Trevor.

"But—"

"The logo will be here when you get back." He places his hands on her shoulders and turns her toward the door.

She circles back toward her desk. "I should get my coat."

"Please, you probably have that thick Utah blood. You'll be fine." He pushes her, and she narrows her eyes at him for a moment.

Why the hell is Trevor so okay with me taking Ande to lunch all by myself?

He doesn't know you've slept with her, asshole, that's why.

I kind of like it that she's kept it a secret. Maybe that means it wasn't just a fling to her.

"Trevor!" She continues her attempt to turn back around, but he keeps pushing her toward the door.

"Go. I have a meeting in ten."

The receptionist, who I never got to introduce myself to, stares at us as though we're a science experiment she doesn't understand, but before long, I'm holding the door open for Ande to walk through.

"Bye," I say with a wave, but Trevor's already gone. "Man, he works fast."

"He's the owner, so he's busy."

We walk down the stairs and I wait until we're out on the sunny sidewalk to continue our conversation. Obviously, Trevor allows casual office attire because she's wearing jeans, all-star Converses, and a shirt that says, "Feed me tacos and everything will be all right."

"When did you move here and how did it come to be?" I ask, following her lead since she obviously has a place in mind. She's charging ahead as if on a mission.

Her head snaps in my direction. "I didn't follow you."

I'm struck silent for a moment. "I didn't think you did."

"It's weird though, right? Here I am living in your city after our fling, and you never knew about it? Makes me seem like a creep." She opens a door at a storefront in the plaza next door and steps inside a restaurant.

I'm wondering what's going on in her head. Why didn't she reach out to me when she got here?

"Ande!" A small man with a gray beard and a pleasant

smile comes out from the back of the restaurant. "Where's Trevor?"

Ande glances at me. "He had to work. I brought a newbie. At least I'm fairly sure he's never had Del Toros before?" She looks at me with questioning eyes.

I shake my head. "I haven't."

"You know I love newbies," the man says to Ande and puts his hand out between us. "I'm Juan."

"Hi, Juan. Cory."

"You look very familiar, Cory. Are you sure you've never been here?"

Ande smiles as though we're hiding a secret.

Although I'm not usually so forthcoming, I decide it appears he's a friend of hers, so there's no sense trying to skirt around the truth. "I play for the Florida Fury."

"The who?" Juan asks, picking up two menus.

"The hockey team," Ande says.

Juan waves me off and gestures at the television mounted to the wall. "It's football here. Sorry."

I laugh but sort of feel like an idiot. I'm sure that impressed Ande. Not.

"I know you like the speedy lunch, so let me get you seated." Juan guides us through the tables to one that faces the street.

We sit down in the booth, Juan placing the menus in front of us, although Ande doesn't pick hers up.

He looks at Ande. "Horchata?"

Her face lights up. "Please."

"And you?"

"I'll just have a water."

Juan's eyebrows furrow and he glances at Ande. "Where did you find this guy? Hockey player and he drinks water over my horchata?"

She laughs, but I feel as though I offended him.

"You didn't let me finish. A water and horchata."

Juan points at me and smiles. "There you go. I'll be right back."

After Juan's gone, Ande leans forward. "You don't have to. I'll drink it if you don't like it."

"It's fine. You come here often?" I look around the small restaurant. There are no more than fifteen tables, mostly tables of two except for two bigger tables in the middle of the restaurant, and a bar along one wall.

"Yeah. And if you wear a T-shirt about tacos, you get one taco free." She grins and points at her T-shirt.

I know it's just a restaurant, but it feels odd she's obviously already made a life in this city. More than me maybe. Which only brings my mind back to my original question. "How did you end up here?"

She leans back in her seat and doesn't say anything for a moment. "I am—"

Juan brings over our drinks and tosses the straws on the table.

"Give us five?" Ande asks.

Juan nods. "You know my lunch rush will be here soon, so five minutes."

After he walks away, she looks at me. "Right after we parted ways, my boss called and said they were closing down the Salt Lake City branch. She put in a transfer for me to come to Florida."

My forehead wrinkles. "And you never reached out to me? I called you."

She pounds her straw on the table and pulls off the paper wrapping before placing the straw in the cup. "Yeah, well... at first it felt weird. I didn't think you'd appreciate hearing that I was moving here and then..." She glances up as though she's already apologizing for what she's about to say. "You seemed to have moved on."

I lean back in my seat, taking the opportunity to free my straw and put it in the drink. "I told you you'd hear rumors."

She nods. "I guess I wasn't expecting that many."

"I understand, but still, I wish you would've reached out."

"It all happened so fast, I couldn't even process it. I left everyone I ever knew for a new job, new city. It was a lot."

I sip the horchata and surprisingly find it delicious. "And now you're with Trevor?"

She sips her drink. "He kind of stole me away from the other company. We met at a conference shortly after I moved here."

I notice she didn't mention their personal relationship. "And you're in graphic design, right?"

Her smile conveys she really loves her job. "Yeah. Not too exciting, just logos and branding for companies. But Trevor puts a lot of trust in me, which means I have a lot more freedom than I did at the last company."

I catch myself studying her every move and hanging on every word. It's been months since I saw her last, yet it's as though no time has passed.

"Okay, five minutes are up. What will it be?" Juan asks, appearing seemingly from nowhere.

Ande doesn't pick up the menu and orders the three-taco special. One chicken, one steak, and one carnitas. Not knowing what's good here, I copy her order.

"I'm going to bring you something special." Juan winks.

After he walks away, I ask Ande, "Do I need to be scared?"

"No, he just loves having new people at his restaurant. The first time Trevor brought me here, I had to spend the rest of my day working with the top button of my jeans undone." She laughs, but the visual triggers memories of her body underneath mine. How she'd squirm when my fingers pushed past her panty line.

It's time I cut to the chase.

"I know you're dating Trevor, but I'd love to remain in contact with you. Go to lunch sometimes, you can come to my games. Trevor seems obsessed with hockey, so I'm sure he wouldn't mind." Although I'd rather have him stay home. "Seems kind of like there was help from the universe to get us in the same city again."

"Sure. Yeah."

It's clear she doesn't really mean it, but I'll take what I can get and bide my time. I'm not wishing she and Trevor won't work out, but hey, if they don't and I'm there to pick up the pieces, where's the harm in that?

I can be her friend even if I go home at night and beat off to memories of fucking her. She doesn't need to know that.

I open my mouth to speak, but Juan comes over with four plates of tacos. "You get one of every kind. That's the only way you'll know what you like best."

I stare at all the plates, wondering if I'll be in any shape to skate tomorrow night.

Ande laughs. "Welcome to the club."

I loved her laugh from the first time I heard it when she stepped on that bus with her friends and couldn't find a seat. It still does something to the pit of my stomach that I can't describe. I might have to help the breakup with Trevor along.

CHAPTER 4

"Jet's gonna get his shot."

Andie

I wait for Trevor outside the Florida Fury arena, not thrilled by the prospect of watching the man I still want to sleep with play all night. Especially after lunch yesterday. He still has that calm demeanor, the one that says he has it all under control. The one that hides his emotions. Although I swear I saw him frown when I mentioned his extracurriculars with the ladies.

"What on earth are you wearing?" I ask Trevor when he approaches. His face is painted black and gray, and he's decked out in an Aiden Drake jersey with a Fury scarf.

"Just a jersey." He looks me over. "You should at least be wearing the team colors."

"You painted your face!"

He nods and smiles as though I should be proud. "Team spirit. You should get some."

Trevor leaves me on the sidewalk and walks toward the entrance. I follow, dodging eye contact from everyone. I'm sure he's not the only one with a painted face, but I don't like the attention he's drawing to us.

He hands the tickets to the attendant, and after a security check, we're let through.

"Want to get food now or later?" Trevor asks.

"I think I need a beer."

I head to the concession stand with Trevor right next to me. "This is so exciting. I never had anyone to go to a hockey game with before. If you get your head out of your ass and start dating Cory, you and I could be up in the suites soon."

I scrunch my eyebrows and look around. "Technically, I'm dating you."

He rocks his head back. "I forgot. Yes, you're my loving girlfriend. Man, I never thought I'd hear myself say those words. Not since I was thirteen at least." He laughs and I order two beers and a pretzel. "And popcorn," Trevor tells the guy behind the counter.

I pay the ransom they extort out of you for food and drink at a professional sporting event, and we carry our snacks into the arena.

"I bet the girlfriends get a discount, or maybe even free snacks," Trevor whispers on our way down the stairs.

"Cool it," I whisper-shout back.

"Go Fury!" some guy says with his hand held up to Trevor. They high-five.

We finally reach the first row, and damn, these are some of the best seats in the house. We're on the side but closer to the goal, and we squeeze past a few people to our seats.

"Love the paint job," the guy sitting next to Trevor says.

"If you're going to be a fan, you might as well go all the way." Trevor makes conversation with the guy.

We've gotten here so early, the teams are still warming up. I narrow my eyes at Trevor, although he's too busy talking to his new friend to notice. I'm sure he did this on purpose.

A tap on the glass in front of me has me whipping my head around to see Cory smiling at me. I wave, feeling heat travel up my cheeks. He looks so different with all his hockey gear on, but not in a bad way.

Trevor bolts up from his seat and fist-bumps him with the glass between them. "Hey, Cory, what's up?"

"Love the face," Cory says, and Trevor gives me a smug look.

I roll my eyes but can't deny it's endearing that he's such a big fan.

Someone else shouts Cory's name from across the ice and he waves goodbye, skating away.

After he leaves, the girl next to me asks, "You know Cory Freeman?"

I glance at her and she's got the cutest blonde pigtails with black and gray ribbons, Cory's number painted on her cheek with glitter. "I do. I mean, not super well, but..."

Time to shut up, since the mom is looking at me as though she thinks I'm his designated puck bunny or something.

The little girl smiles wide. "He went to my dad's college, so when he got traded here, he became my favorite."

"That's nice of you."

She looks beyond me at Trevor. "Everyone loves Shamrock, and I get it, he's good. He was my favorite until they drafted Jet."

I'm trying to keep up with her use of the players' nicknames.

"Once Jet gets his shot at first line, he'll show everyone how he got that nickname."

I chuckle. "You know a lot about this sport, huh?"

Her mom nods. "No dolls or Barbies for this one."

"I'm Ava." She puts out her hand, and I shake it.

"Ande."

Her eyes flare for a moment, but she's quick to recover. "Do you know all the players?"

I smile. "Not really. I've met some of them a time or two."

"I tried to get into Cory's meet and greet a few months ago, but I didn't get a ticket. Maybe if they do it again, I'll get lucky." She sips her soft drink.

"So your dad doesn't know Cory?" I ask.

She shakes her head. "No, they just went to the same school."

"Years apart," her mom says, which makes sense. I figure this girl is about eleven.

"The next time I see Cory, I'll tell him about you," I say. "Do you come to a lot of games?"

"No. This is for my birthday. My parents got me tickets as a present."

A man I assume is her father makes his way down the row with trays of snacks, and a young boy in front of him is barreling past everyone. He tells the boy to slow down. The mom rises from her seat and helps. The little guy takes her seat, and she moves down.

The man takes the seat beside Ava and whispers, "You're not supposed to talk to strangers."

"She's not a stranger. She knows Jet."

The little boy's eyes light up like Santa himself just walked into the arena. "What's he like?"

"Very nice actually." I smile at him.

"Here, kids, eat your food." The mom passes out the food to everyone.

I've been so busy chatting with Ava that I didn't notice the players are now off the ice. Trevor finally decides to grant me some attention and we chat for a few minutes. The direction of our conversation turns when I ask how much these seats probably cost.

Trevor shakes his head. "A shit ton. I once looked into season tickets—thought I'd put them through the company, maybe give some out on occasion. It was insane."

The lights go out in the arena, and Ava grabs my arm. "It's starting."

They announce the starting lineup and Cory isn't a part of it, but I'm familiar with a lot of people on the line. Drake sets up in the middle and gets the puck first, shooting it to Ford, who takes it down the ice near us.

Ava gets up from her seat. "Let's go, Richie! Shoot it to your bestie!"

Man, she really does keep up with the gossip of this team. But Ford, a.k.a. Richie, shoots it back to Drake, a.k.a. Shamrock, and he passes to Warner, a.k.a. Ford's bestie. The puck somehow goes back to Ford, then to Warner right before the red buzzer lights up.

Ava's hands go up in the air and she pounds on the glass. I look next to me and see Trevor banging even harder on the glass. Warner skates around the net, approaching our section and winks at Trevor, then he gives Ava a high five on the partition.

Her eyes light up and she turns to her parents. "Did you see that?"

Her mom holds up her phone. "Got a picture."

Ava picks up her pretzel and sits back down next to me. "Warner is so dreamy, but he's engaged to Ford's sister."

I shake my head and chuckle. "Please tell me what hockey blog you follow." Because seriously, that engagement just happened.

The game is going by pretty fast, and I'm surprised to find that I'm enjoying myself.

When there's a break in play, Ava rises up on her knees and whispers, "I know who you are. It's okay, I won't tell my mom. It's the part of the game she doesn't like me to know about."

I somehow manage to stop my mouth from hanging

open and keep my eyes from bulging out of my face. She's kidding, right?

"I read the stuff about Jet, but I don't believe it. He's just spreading oats is what my dad says."

I swallow past the dryness of my throat with the beer in my hand. I'll use anything to change the subject, so I point at the ice. "Oh look, here they come again."

Sure enough, Drake has the puck, headed in our direction. He shoots it to Ford, who quickly loses it to the defender but is able to knock it free. Drake skates to retrieve it, but a player from the other team slams him into the boards in a way that looks awkward and probably painful. Drake slides to the ice and doesn't move.

"You fucker!" Maksim comes out of nowhere and grabs the other player's jersey.

"Now this is what I love," Trevor says next to me, getting closer to the glass.

Everyone does, eager to see how Drake is doing. The Jumbotron shows a motionless Drake slumped on the ice while both teams go after one another.

A medic team rushes onto the ice, and the camera scans the wives and girlfriends' section until it finds Saige running down the stairs with Tedi behind her. They reach the glass at the end of the stairs. Saige has tears in her eyes and is biting her fingernails while Tedi tries to console her.

Meanwhile, the refs try to get control of the situation on the ice. Maksim breaks away from the opponent he was fighting, skates over to Drake, and kneels beside him, but soon a stretcher is wheeled out.

The entire arena is quiet as we watch Aiden get put on the stretcher and taken out. Saige joins him as they head off the ice—to an ambulance, I presume. Aiden gives the audience a wave, but it's clear he's hurt. Still, everyone present claps to let him know we're behind him.

"Ava, dear?" Her mom touches Ava to check on her, but the little girl seems fine.

"Jet's gonna get his shot." She's quick to look at me. "Not that I hope anything is wrong with Shamrock."

"I know." I can't help the tears that have welled in my own eyes. My heart breaks for Saige and Aiden. I can't imagine how scared she is right now.

But Ava was right—Cory got moved up and is on the first line now. When he skates out, the crowd cheers for him. He doesn't disappoint, scoring two goals by the time the game is over.

I wonder what that's like for him? To come in after a teammate is injured.

After the game is over, Cory skates over to the glass, takes off his glove, and holds up a piece of paper that reads, *"Meet me after. Follow the bunnies."*

I nod mostly because Trevor wouldn't let me say no anyway. Then I look at Ava and her family packing up. I tried to get Cory to at least say hello to her, but he got called away immediately.

"Wait," I say to Ava's mom. "Cory and the guys will be at Carmelo's after the game. At least some of them will. Though I'm not sure what's going on now that Aiden is hurt. I can't promise anything, but if you come, I'm sure we can get her a few pictures and autographs."

The mom looks at the dad a little reluctantly.

Trevor butts into our conversation. "This is once-in-a-lifetime stuff. Who cares about bedtimes?"

"Says the man who has no kids," I deadpan.

But the parents nod and thank me, never giving me an answer.

Meanwhile, Trevor and I follow the bunnies to the area the players must come after the games. Rumor is, Aiden has a concussion and went to the hospital, but he's okay. He'll be out for a while. I don't know how this information gets passed around so quickly.

Cory comes out of the arena later than everyone and I wonder if he had to do interviews since he was the big player tonight. He ignores all the women clamoring for his attention and walks over to Trevor and me.

"I hate that I got my chance to shine because my team-mate was hurt," he says, his head hanging low.

"I heard he's okay, a concussion?" I bite my lip, seeing the conflict in Cory's eyes.

He nods. "I might go see him at the hospital."

I didn't even notice him come out the door, but Kane appears beside Cory and slaps him on the back. "No, you're not. He's probably got his eyes shut in a dark room right now and been told he shouldn't have any stimulation. He needs to rest right now. Believe me, Drake would want you to celebrate. You didn't check him out there. It's not your fault. We're going to Carmelo's!"

The group roars and it seems Trevor believes he's part of them because he's right next to Kane Burrows, leading the pack. Lord help me.

CHAPTER 5

Andie

"**H**as he ever met a stranger?" Cory asks me once we're out of his sports car and walking through the parking lot toward Carmelo's.

He's referring to Trevor, who is officially the worst pretend boyfriend ever. He keeps ditching me to hang with the players. He left me to catch a ride with Cory while he jumped into Kane's giant truck.

"He's really outgoing." I give him a wane smile.

Cory leans in closer and the scent of his cologne fills my nostrils. What is it about a freshly showered man that gets me so hot? "I'm assuming he doesn't know about us?"

Please tell me he didn't ask me that. I don't want to lie to the man, so I try to be discreet. "He knows how we met, but I didn't give him all the details."

It's technically true. I didn't give any details when Trevor asked how big Cory is. Trevor knows no boundaries.

"That surprises me."

I tilt my head and frown. "Why?"

"Because he's cool with me taking you to lunch and driving you over here tonight."

All valid. I bite my cheek, unsure how to answer. "He's not the jealous type."

"Wish I could say the same. It might sound offside, but if

you were my girl, I wouldn't let you get in a car with a guy you fucked for a week on vacation." He glances at me and my skin pricks with awareness.

"I guess he trusts me."

Cory laughs. "He should trust you. It's everyone else he shouldn't."

The large crowd goes into Carmelo's, and it's then I remember Ava and her family.

"Oh shit," I say.

"What?"

I stop walking. "You might be mad at me because I'm pretty sure the minute you walk into Carmelo's, people will be wanting to celebrate your game, but I did something."

He looks at me with both eyebrows raised.

"Did you see the little girl next to me at the game? She had your number painted on her cheeks."

His head moves back and forth like maybe he remembers.

"Anyway, she's a huge fan of yours. I guess her dad and you went to the same college. It's her birthday, so her parents bought her first-row tickets to the game. I might have told them you hang out here after the games and she might be waiting for you to get an autograph or a picture." I bite my lip. I'm sure this is no place for Ava or her brother. Why did I suggest it in the first place?

"Oh cool, let's go surprise her then." He nods and walks toward the door.

"Seriously? It might put a damper on the night..."

"No, it won't. I've never had a young fan before. I'm kind of stoked." He opens Carmelo's door and the noise is so loud it billows out like a cloud of smoke. He motions for me to walk in ahead of him. "Let's go."

I pick up my pace and walk through the door. Trevor is

seated in a round booth with Kane, Tweetie, and a few others. Maksim and Ford aren't here. Maksim is probably at the hospital and Ford has a daughter, so maybe he's not into this scene anymore?

What is clear is that there are puck bunnies everywhere. I don't get a chance to give that much thought before I hear my name called. I turn to see Ava's family in a booth away from the players. Both parents look unsure about being here.

Cory steps up to them right away. "Which of you is Ava?"

Ava stares at him in awe and raises her hand. Cory puts his hand up for a high five and she slaps it with a huge grin.

After shaking both parents' hands and introducing himself, he ruffles the younger brother's hair and surprises me when he asks, "Is there room for me?"

Ava quickly slides over. "Ande too."

She's so cute I can't tell her no, so with a glance at Trevor —who hasn't even looked this way—I slide in, leaving us all cramped in the booth.

"We can't forget Ande," Cory says, his hand squeezing my thigh under the table.

Electricity zings up my thigh to hit the bull's-eye between my legs. It takes me a second to remember that a good girlfriend wouldn't like another man putting his hands on her, so I slide as far away from him as I can manage, which isn't far at all.

Cory talks with her about his two goals, and he assures her that Aiden will be back on the ice soon.

When the waitress comes over, Cory leans over me, which means his arm is extended around my shoulders. How much more will I be tested tonight? I'm failing miserably.

I smile when he asks for a full cake with candles for Ava.

"So sweet," I whisper. I thought Cory would give Ava his autograph and take a picture, but I didn't expect him to spend his whole night with her and her family.

Once we've all gotten more comfortable with one another, Ava's mom asks, "Are you two a couple?"

Cory looks at me. "Should I tell them, or should you?"

I shake my head.

"No, Mom, they aren't," Ava answers for him.

"How do you know?" she asks with a wrinkled forehead, looking at her daughter.

Ava shrugs and grins at me sheepishly, clearly asking me not to tell on her for reading gossip blogs. "Everyone knows Cory is single."

Her mom looks at Cory and he nods in confirmation. "Ande is dating Trevor." He thumbs in his direction.

"The face-paint guy?" she asks me with raised eyebrows.

"That's him." I need to work on my enthusiasm.

"Oh." She looks at Trevor again and back at me.

I don't even want to know what he's doing. I wouldn't be surprised if he's dancing on the table or something.

"Jet!" Kane screams over the music from the other side of the room.

"We should let you get back to your friends," Ava's dad says, pulling out his wallet.

Cory holds up his hand. "Please, it's on me, and I'll be right back."

He squeezes my thigh again for me to slide out of the booth first. When I do, he goes over and talks to the waitress, then Kane and the rest of the players.

"This was so nice of you to set up, Ande. Thank you." Ava's mom puts her hand over mine.

"No problem. I honestly had no idea he would be so forthcoming. It's nice to see."

We share a smile. Some athletes are rumored to be complete dicks to their fans.

The restaurant lights dim and Cory, Warner, Tweetie, and Kane all walk over singing "Happy Birthday" to Ava. Cory holds a chocolate cake with lit candles. Her eyes bulge out and they all urge her to blow out the candles and make a wish.

We end up celebrating with milk and chocolate cake. Before Ava's family leaves, Imogen gets their number, handing over her business card, and tells them that a special gift will be coming. Ava's last request was to get a picture taken with Cory, which he happily obliged.

After the family leaves, I can't get the smile off my face.

"So, can we give up the jig or what?" Trevor whispers in my ear.

"No!" I whisper-shout. "Why would you ask that?"

"Because you have that lovesick look in your eye. You obviously want him."

I consider what he's saying while I look at Cory clinking a shot glass with Kane and Tweetie before tossing it back. "I do not. It's just nice to see how happy Ava was, that's all."

"Who's Ava?" He bites the cherry off his toothpick.

"Seriously? Do you have any idea what is going on around you?"

"Well, it's hard to concentrate when there are this many big, burly men around. I'd be getting laid right now if I didn't have to pretend to be your other half."

I guffaw. "By whom?"

He looks around the restaurant. "Statistics say that one of these players is probably in the closet. Maybe Kane? All those years in the league and he's never settled down. Kinda suspicious."

I roll my eyes.

"Plus, that guy we sat next to was giving me the look."

"You think everyone gives you the look." I sip my wine.

"Have you looked at me?" He gestures from his face to his abdomen.

I laugh and quickly swallow my wine before it dribbles out of my mouth. "One thing's for sure, no one can shake your self-confidence."

"No, and they shouldn't be able to do it to you either." He eyes Cory.

"It's a lot of things." I twist the wineglass around by the stem.

"It's that ex-dipshit-boyfriend you told me about. Look." Trevor turns to face me. "I was totally on your side after reading about Cory being a douche and sleeping with a lot of women, but now that I've been with him a few times, it's clear he only has eyes for you. I think you should explore it."

I shake my head before he even finishes. "You don't get it. My insecurities alone would ruin everything. Some people can handle a relationship with someone in the public eye. I'm not one of them."

Cory nods at me to come join him, but a puck bunny slides to the side that should be open for me. Jealousy stokes anger inside me, only confirming that I'm right. I'd end up being some crazy bitch if I dated Cory. He's not the guy to get me over the insecurity that my next boyfriend will cheat on me just like my old one did. I need a sweet, kind man who isn't being propositioned every minute.

"You're delusional. I'm gonna go call Vinny." Trevor walks away to call his fuck buddy, which means I'll be finding my own way home tonight. Which is fine. I'm actually ready to go right now.

"It's hard, right?" Imogen comes up next to me and sits beside me at the bar.

"What is?"

"The whole puck bunny thing." She looks at Cory and Kane, who are being entertained by two women flirting with them. Though neither of them looks that into it.

"It's not my concern." I point at Trevor, who's by himself in the corner on his cell. "That's my guy."

"Oh yeah, Trevor. I keep forgetting you have a boyfriend. You and Cory were so hot and heavy on the island. How come nothing came of it after?"

I got to know the girls a little while I was on vacation, but they're all obviously close-knit. Without Sophie and Brit here, Trevor's been my main source of advice.

"It was a vacation fling." I shrug.

She nods and brings what I think is sparkling water to her lips. "Funny, Warner looks at me the same way Cory does you, and it's not a fling with us."

I laugh. "You're really drilling down, huh?"

"I'm the Florida Fury hype girl. I have to know where the players are at. I can't offer Cory up on a date if he's taken." She waits for my response, her gaze never leaving mine.

"Well, as far as I know, he's single."

Trevor comes over. "Ready to go?"

I finish my wine and slide off the barstool. "Yep. Good to see you," I say to Imogen.

"You two are leaving?" Her eyes scour the room, and I follow the direction of her gaze when it stops. Warner sits at a table alone, his head down as though he's nodded off. "He didn't even want to come tonight, but I told him he has to be a team player, congratulate Cory on his game. He'd rather us be at home."

"Doesn't sound like a problem to me." I eye Cory, who's taking another shot with Kane. The two puck bunnies are more in a conversation with themselves but lingering close in case their presence is requested.

"I'm gonna go wake him up. Have a great night, guys." She weaves through the crowd to Warner, taps him on the shoulder, and kisses his cheek. He jolts and smiles, rising from the booth the minute he sees she's ready.

"Vinny's coming to get me, so you have a few minutes to say goodbye to Cory," Trevor says.

"He looks busy. I'll text him once I'm in my Uber."

"Want me to ask Vinny to drop you at home?"

"Nah." I pull up the app and order the Uber. It should be here in only a few minutes.

"You sure?"

I nod. "Let's go."

Trevor and I make our escape. I kiss him on the cheek and thank him for coming, reminding him to remove his makeup before he and Vinny get too hot and heavy tonight.

He chuckles as we say our goodbyes. I'm in the Uber when the door of Carmelo's opens and Cory steps out. My car is pulling away and thankfully has tinted windows, but his disappointed gaze travels to Trevor, who's getting into Vinny's car with a kiss hello.

Damn it, Trevor!

Worst fake boyfriend ever.

CHAPTER 6

Cory

Finding my way into the corporate offices at the Fury arena, I follow the directions Warner gave me to Imogen's office. She has no secretary, so I knock on the door.

"Come in," she says.

I walk in and there's no surprise on her face—I assume because Warner told her the minute I left him after practice.

"Hey, Cory." She smiles.

"Hey."

She stands and slips back into her heels, then walks over to sit in one of the two chairs on the other side of her desk.

"You don't have to get up for me."

She waves off my concern. "I hate the formality of a desk between people. Maybe because almost every discussion I had with my father growing up had a big desk between us. Anyway..." She shrugs. "What's up?"

I sit in the chair next to her and my fingers wring together in knots. There are few women in my life besides my mom. I'm an only child and we weren't all that close to our extended family. It's hard finding women who are truly just interested in being your friend. I fell for that twice and broke both their hearts. Not the best feeling in the world.

"Sorry to just barge in here, but... I want to talk about Ande."

Her head rocks back and she smiles. "What about Ande?"

"Imogen," I say her name with little patience because I'm not one to play games. She knows I want Ande.

"Okay, I'm sorry, I'm just a romantic and wanted to hear the words. You hockey boys always keep your emotions inside. I want to shake you up until you confess." She waves it off. "She has a boyfriend, right?"

"That's the thing. I'm trying to be respectful of her boyfriend, but it's getting harder to do. Trevor is awesome and he's also her boss."

"Boss, really?"

I nod.

"Sticky situation."

"That's the thing. I've never seen them kiss, never seen them show physical intimacy to one another. And the other night at Carmelo's, they took different cars home."

She shrugs. "Maybe they live in opposite directions, and one had an important event the next day?"

I shake my head. "Trevor got in the passenger seat of another guy's car and kissed him hello... on the lips."

"Huh. Well, he's a friendly guy..."

I raise my eyebrows and stare at her until she's laughing.

"Okay, so why are you up here talking to me?"

Warner walks in, drops his stuff, and goes to her desk chair in front of her computer, reclining and closing his eyes. "Just ignore me."

"Warner, you have to wait outside," Imogen says.

"No, I don't. Do I, Jet?"

I shrug. "I asked him first. He suggested I talk to you."

She shakes her head at Warner as he rests his linked hands on his stomach and continues to keep his eyes closed.

"That's why I'm up here. He couldn't help me, and I didn't want to ask Kane since he always seems a little sour when it comes to relationships."

Imogen nods. "That's because Kane and Jana are doing the nasty and not telling anyone."

Warner peeks one eye open. "Don't start rumors, babe."

"I'm not." She turns her attention back to me. "It's solely my gut feeling, but I'm not buying the whole 'I hate you' vibe they try to put off." She pats my thigh. "But we're here to talk about you."

"She has a hard time staying on track," Warner says, chuckling.

"You just lie over there and sleep."

I don't want to sound like a girl, but they're cute together. It's the kind of relationship I've always imagined myself having with my someday wife. Joking, loving, hot.

He winks at her and shifts in her chair to get comfortable.

"I can't call her out without more proof," I say to Imogen.

"Well, the first question you have to ask yourself is why you want to call her out in the first place. Say Trevor isn't her boyfriend. Why do you care?"

"I thought that was clear."

"It is," Warner says. "Gen doesn't play games. We all know Jet wants in Ande's pants again."

She leans back and crosses her arms, looking at me. "I want to hear it from you. I have to know your heart is in this too, not just your dick."

"This has to do with all the damn gossip?" I scowl at her.

She taps her perfectly manicured nail against her

glossed lips. "Is it gossip? You *are* sleeping with numerous women."

I adamantly shake my head. "First of all, I'm single, so it's no one's business. Second of all, that was until I found Ande again in that grocery store."

"So no women after that?" She holds out her hand with her pinkie extended.

I stare at her hand, and she waits until I pinkie swear her.

"If this makes you feel better." I wrap my large digit around hers.

After our pinkies shake, she seems appeased, leaning back in her chair again. "We need to see how they interact without you around."

"Exactly, but I'm the connection. There's no reason for them to be around you guys if I'm not there."

We sit in silence for a minute while Imogen and I think.

"Seriously?" Warner sits up in his chair.

"What?" Imogen's forehead wrinkles.

"Trevor loves hockey. Give them another set of tickets but have them sit in the wives and girlfriends' section. Imogen and the rest of the ladies can report back."

Imogen's mouth hangs open and she points at him. "That scares me."

He chuckles. "What does?"

"Your manipulating skills."

"How do you think I got you?" He winks and smiles, leaning back in the chair.

She tosses a paper clip at him and it lands right on his stomach.

"Sounds like a good enough option," I say.

"Yes, and can I say how annoyed I am that I didn't come up with it?" Imogen rounds her desk, placing her hands on her husband's jean-clad legs and separating them to make room for her.

He perks up, his hands going to her hips and drawing her in.

"And that's my cue. Have a great night, guys." I stand and wave, walking out of her office.

"Lock the door on your way out," Warner says.

Imogen laughs. "No, don't do that, Cory."

I press the bottom button because hell, if that was Ande and me, I'd want the door locked too.

THREE NIGHTS LATER, we have a home game. Instead of hand-delivering tickets to Ande and Trevor, I opted for courier service.

Trevor messaged me right away and thanked me, saying they'd be there.

Now, I'm lacing up my skates with the feeling of being dishonest sitting in my gut like a rock. I should just ask her what's really up. Why am I playing games?

Because she obviously thinks I'm the douche the hockey gossip blogs say I am.

"Need to speak to you, Freeman," Coach Vittner calls from his office.

"You know what this is about, right?" Ford razzes me from across the room.

There are two things it could be about. The fact that Drake hasn't returned to the lineup yet or the fact that an article came out today about professional athletes who use their fame to get women. It's true, but the article failed to mention that very often, women are offering themselves up.

I walk across the locker room into Coach's office.

"Sit down, Freeman." He signals to the chair in front of his desk.

"Is there a problem?"

"Drake is out for the rest of the week. Then they'll reevaluate him. So, you're the man of the hour. Need you to step up."

I nod, nervous energy thrumming through my veins. "I'm your guy, Coach."

He sits in his chair and peels an orange. "I don't think you need me to tell you how to handle this responsibility. Word came from upstairs that you need a talking-to, but I'm not your fucking daddy. You've got one of those, so do both of us a favor and keep it in your pants. Or if you can't handle that, for Christ's sake, Freeman, pick women who will keep it discreet."

"I'm not—"

He's quick to raise his hand. "I don't need to know. Just keep your name out of the fucking blogs. I don't care much where you guys get your dicks wet as long as you're on the ice when I tell you to be and you're ready to give me your all. I understand what the first couple years are like when you're getting all the attention from the broads. But you're on first line now and getting more ice time. You were always grounded, Freeman, it's one reason I wanted you. Don't make me regret my decision."

I feel as though there's a giant lump in my throat, and I swallow past it. "I won't, Coach."

He throws the peels from his orange in the trash and stares at me for a moment. "That's all. Now go."

I stand and hesitate, thinking I should promise him or tell him I'll make him proud. But he continues to eat his orange, reading an article in the newspaper.

"You need an invitation? Get your ass on the ice for warm-ups."

"Yes, Coach." I walk out of the office and some of the guys are already gone. Kane is still at his locker though, and I get the feeling he might be waiting for me.

"You still on starting line?" he asks, putting on his goalie pads.

"Yeah."

"Good. See you out there. And I heard about your little plan. Word to the wise—don't let yourself get distracted over a woman. They aren't worth it." He pats me on the back.

I turn to leave the locker room and find Jana Gerhardt standing there with a look like she wishes she had a machete to cut into Kane's head like a coconut.

"Miss Gerhardt," I say and dodge by her, putting on my helmet and gloves on my way down the hall.

I skate onto the ice and ignore Kane's advice, looking in the direction of the girlfriends and wives' area. Trevor and Ande aren't there yet, but neither are a lot of the wives.

Getting involved in the warm-ups, Ford, Warner, and I practice our shots and passes to one another. I love playing with them. They're talented players, and since they figured out their shit, our wins have tripled. The playoffs are still a long shot though.

Warner skids to a stop next to me. "My girl is on a mission now."

"How so?"

"For you to get Ande, and do you know what that means for me?" From his tone, I'm guessing it's not good. "It means I'm not the center of her attention. I like being the center of her attention, Jet."

Ford laughs. "Just wait until you have a baby. Goodbye,

Warner; hello, baby." He waves mockingly at Warner and skates away.

Warner skates after him and Kane finally comes out onto the ice. The ref makes a joke about Kane's age and knee replacements. Kane slides into his place in front of the net and it's clear he's no longer in a good mood. I think about what Imogen said about Jana and Kane. No way. They couldn't be more opposite. She's always sniping at him every time I see them speaking, and he practically growls back at her.

After warm-ups, we leave the rink. Ford, the alternate captain, gives us a pep talk to get us going. When the starting lineup is announced, I find Trevor and Ande up in the stands. Trevor's face isn't painted and Ande's talking to Tedi more than Trevor.

It isn't until the second period, when I'm on the bench during a commercial break and the kiss cam goes around the arena, that I'm drawn back to them again. The camera stays steady on Ande, and she notices before Trevor.

He looks at her and she at him. They look uncomfortable, but Ande presses her lips to Trevor's, who stays still, not moving. The kiss couldn't be more platonic, which brings a smile to my face.

"That was my idea," Imogen says from behind me.

"Imogen Jacobs, get off my bench!" Coach Vittner shouts.

She ignores him. "Great idea, right?"

"Don't make me say it again," Coach says, stepping closer to us.

"Leaving now, Coach! But there's your answer, Cory. Figure out your next step." She claps and kisses the top of Warner's head. "You look awesome as usual out there. Love you."

"Imogen!" Coach screams.

"Going. Going. Jeez." She walks away and the kiss cam moves on to another couple.

"Hey, Imogen." I lean back so I can see her, and she turns around. "Thanks."

She smiles and nods.

Now the question is, what am I going to do with my newfound knowledge?

CHAPTER 7

"Ride with me to Carmelo's?"
Cory

Andie

"**Y**ou could've tried harder," I whisper after the kiss cam stops stalking us.

"Gimme a break. I haven't kissed a girl since I was forced to for a bet in the seventh grade." He munches his popcorn, his cheeks red as tomatoes.

"Sorry," I mumble. I should never have put him in this position.

"Don't be. You weren't that bad, but I'm not switching teams because of it."

Tedi comes and sits in front of us, a fresh pretzel and nacho cheese in her lap. "Something is up with you two. I mean, you're both twentysomethings and you never touch." She waves her salt-covered pretzel at us.

"I'm in my thirties," Trevor says.

She gives him the once-over. "Give me the name and number of your plastic surgeon."

They both laugh, but my gaze is focused on the rink. The Fury are ahead, so Cory isn't playing as much as earlier in the game. I'm assuming that's so he can save some energy and not risk him being injured along with Aiden. For some reason, I swear I can feel Cory's gaze on me from the bench.

While Trevor and Tedi joke around about Botox and lip injections, I'm struck with the realization that pretending

Trevor is my boyfriend was the stupidest idea I've probably ever had.

Imogen returns and sits next to me. "So, that wasn't exactly what we're looking for with the kiss cam." She laughs and knocks my arm.

"We kissed, and it was very uncomfortable. I'm not big on public affection. I can't even believe they still do that thing in this day and age." God, I sound like I have a stick up my ass.

Imogen waits for me to say anything else, but I don't.

"Can I ask you a real question?"

It's clear by her tone what she's going to ask, so I answer with a firm, "No."

"Okay." She leans back and crosses her legs. She's all decked out in spirit wear for Florida Fury. Even has cute number thirty-four earrings.

"I like your earrings," I say, with the hope that it detours our conversation away from my not-so-real relationship with Trevor, and also because I legit like them.

She touches her ears. "Thanks. Warner got them for me. The guys have some stupid competition about who can deck out their woman with the most fan gear. Lena!" she calls, and Lena turns around. She's without Annabelle tonight. "Show Ande your sweatshirt."

Laughing, Lena stands and unzips her jacket.

"Did he bedazzle that himself?" Tedi shouts and everyone laughs.

Lena shakes her head. "You'd think, right?" She rolls her eyes and sits back down.

"See? Of course Warner and my brother compete extra hard. I'm pretty sure Lena and I will be embarrassed to come to a game at some point. So far, Warner's been tasteful, but the ideas will stop coming and I'm going to end up wearing a sweatshirt like Lena's."

I shrug. "It wasn't that bad."

"Are you kidding me? There's a reason she has a jacket on."

We both laugh.

"Well, I better get going. We're having musical chairs during the intermission. Cory is going to make a surprise entrance, so make sure you check him out." She coyly grins at me and walks up the stairway.

I shake my head as though she's delusional, but she's clearly picked up on the whole fake relationship. My heart beats harder. Have we been pretending for nothing? Do all these women know? I must seem like the biggest fool, making up a relationship when they saw the connection Cory and I had in the tropics. And if they know, does Cory? Has he been playing with me?

I groan.

"Why are you as white as a ghost?" Trevor cozies up to me.

"Does everyone know?" I lean in and whisper, being sure no one else hears me.

He cringes. The same cringe he gave me when I wore light-gray pants during my period and leaked during a client meeting. Without knowing, I stood and showed them out of the office. Embarrassing as hell.

I bury my head in my hands. "I'm an idiot, aren't I?"

He pulls my hands away from my face. "You're not an idiot, and I doubt they *all* know."

I let out a long sigh. I can't blame Trevor. He did the best he could, and it wasn't fair for me to ask him in the first place. "It's time I face the fact that I should've been truthful from the get-go."

The buzzer rings through the arena, alerting us that period two is over. A crew rushes onto the ice with huge inflatable chairs, and Imogen follows with a microphone to entertain the crowd that hasn't already gone for a bathroom break or to get food.

"Hello, Florida Fury family!" she shouts into the microphone and people cheer. "We need to make this quick because I secretly stole one of the players to help us judge this contest and we need to get him back before Coach Vittner knows he's gone. Got it?"

Hoots and hollers ring through the arena. Then the crowd screams Warner's number.

"Thirty-four!" they chant over and over.

I'm not sure if they suspect it'll be Warner because of his very public devotion to his new wife or if it's just who they want. Not long after their engagement, Warner and Imogen rushed off to get married and had a small ceremony with just their immediate family present.

"Sorry to disappoint, but my hubby isn't who's joining us. Put your hands together for our center, Cory Freeman!"

Cory skates out with his helmet off, waving at the crowd and looking as delicious as ever. I can't help but picture all the ink on his tawny skin under his jersey.

The crowd cheers, but they aren't as loud as they were when they were chanting Warner's jersey number. My heart tugs for Cory, remembering one of the nights at the resort when he opened up to me on how hard it was to be one of the few Black players in the NHL. I know he wants so badly to be on top and show his community what's possible.

"And for our lovely contestants." Imogen holds her hand out as five people walk onto the carpet that's been draped over the ice.

"Who would sign up for this?" Trevor says.

"Today's winner will get breakfast with Cory and be able to ask any burning questions they might have," Imogen announces.

"Now I would," Trevor says.

I eye the two women in the group of five who are looking at Cory as though they'd enjoy more than just breakfast with him, and jealousy sticks to my skin like a burr. My hope is that the middle-aged bald man wins.

Although I will say, Cory doesn't seem to pay the women any extra attention. He shouts "Go!" into the microphone and all five of the contestants walk in a slow circle around the inflatable chairs. The music plays and the crowd cheers.

The music stops and they all descend on the inflatable chairs. The middle-aged guy is snug in his and the college kid grabs one right in front of the two women. One woman slides into a chair before the elderly woman can reach it and is met with boos from the crowd. Then the last girl lunges. I give her credit for her effort, but the chair goes flying across the ice. She moves to chase it and Cory skates over, grabbing it right before the woman reaches it and almost falls if not for Cory there to save her. And by saving her, I mean he has the inflatable chair in one hand and one arm under her rib cage, his hand dangerously close to her breast.

"What a prince." Trevor waves himself.

I resist the temptation of looking at him and rolling my eyes.

Cory gets her secured in the seat and he hugs the elderly woman goodbye since she's out of the game.

I watch the rest of the rounds, thankful each time the middle-aged guy wins a seat. Forgetting myself, I jump up at the end and cheer. Trevor and Tedi both raise a skeptical eyebrow at me.

I feel my cheeks heat. "What?"

"For someone with a boyfriend, you seem pretty happy the guy won," Tedi says and laughs.

I sit down in my chair and pick up my beer, guzzling a healthy amount.

Cory skates back to the locker room. When the buzzer rings a little more than ten minutes later, the third period begins. The Fury end up defeating the other team with a score of three to two.

"On to Carmelo's!" Tedi raises her hand in the air and hops up from her seat.

From what I've gathered, Tedi and Tweetie party hard, although they do it together. The few hockey blogs I've read say that Tedi's the only woman he's ever committed to and that he's actually faithful to her.

"I think we're going to head out," I say, and Trevor gives me his puppy-dog face. "We have that meeting first thing in the morning." I give him the eye, but he pretends not to notice and waves me off.

"They're longtime clients. We can go for a little bit."

"Can I speak to you for a moment?" I ask through clenched teeth.

We walk far enough away from Tedi that she won't overhear.

"Trevor, the kiss cam gave us up. I can't see Cory right now. He was on the bench and saw it all." My stomach lurches at the thought of seeing him, and my anxiety spikes. All I want to do is retreat back to my house.

"No one knows anything unless we tell them." He shrugs.

I stare at him, saying nothing.

"One drink and I'll stick by your side the entire time." He raises his hand for a pinkie swear.

With a long sigh, I wrap my pinkie around his and agree

to one drink. Only because he's been such a good friend to even accommodate my stupid request to pretend to be my boyfriend in the first place.

We head back over to Tedi, and the three of us walk out and around the arena to meet the players where all the fans congregate. Most of them are puck bunnies hoping for some action tonight.

Aiden Drake is first to leave, because he's not playing at the moment. He swings his arm around Saige, and he smiles at me when he leaves. "Your boy is doing great. By the time I'm cleared, I'll be knocked down a line."

I don't bother correcting him that Cory isn't my guy.

Saige shakes her head but shoots me an expression to say I shouldn't worry about Aiden.

One by one, the players come out, and even though I've been giving myself a mental pep talk while I wait, I'm still not prepared when Cory saunters out. The sight of him fills me with nerves and anticipation. Until the group of women swarm him like a cluster of bees to a sunflower. Then I'm just filled with irritation.

Kane shakes his head and comes over to us. "You guys heading to Carmelo's?"

"Why aren't they all over you?" I ask.

He laughs. "Because I'm the old guy. He's the hotshot right now." He nods toward Cory, who peeks over the crowd of women at me.

There's absolutely no way I can handle being with someone who's put in front of temptation all the time like a professional athlete. Not after Michael.

"You're not old," Trevor says. "You're distinguished. Like a smooth scotch. Cory's like a tequila shot off the body."

They both laugh.

"They taste different, but they're both delicious just the same," Trevor continues.

Jana walks out of the office area entrance, stealing Kane's attention. She stops and looks at us.

"I'm gonna head over to Carmelo's. No reason to hang around here." Kane straightens up and walks across the parking lot. He doesn't stop to talk to Jana, but heads directly to his truck. Jana does the same to her Mercedes-Maybach.

"We should head over too," I say.

"We've waited this long." Trevor approaches the group. "Sorry to interrupt, ladies, but I'm stealing Prince Charming away."

They all boo, but to my surprise, Trevor successfully pulls Cory out of the middle of the women. When I'm face to face with Cory, the breath rushes from my lungs. He is so good-looking with his full lips and strong jaw, and I feel drawn to him. Then I look behind him at all the women watching him.

"I need to talk to you. Ride with me to Carmelo's?" he asks, then glances at Trevor. "You don't mind, do you?"

"Not at all."

I widen my eyes at Trevor. "I came with Trevor so it would probably be rude..." I say mostly to Trevor, with the tone that says he should step in and save me.

He slaps Cory on the back. "You're in good hands. See you two over there."

And he walks away, leaving me with Cory and a few dozen eyes staring at me.

Thanks a lot, *boyfriend.*

CHAPTER 8

"We need to amp up this party!"

Cory

I open the passenger door so Ande can slide into my sports car and shut the door behind her. As I round the front of my car, I'm hoping I don't offend her with the questions I intend to ask, but as I open my door, my phone chirps with a text message. I pull it out to deal with that so there'll be no other interruptions during our conversation. I assume it's my parents texting to tell me good game, but then I see the name on the screen.

York: *Just a friendly reminder that I'm coming into town.*

I completely forgot I have to nip that in the ass. Now that Ande is back in my life, I have no interest in seeing her again, which I've tried to make clear every time she's texted me since I saw Ande in that grocery store. I've been trying to be polite without being rude, so I try to continue on the same way, hoping she'll take a hint.

Me: *Let me know if you want tickets for a game.*

York: *I already told you I don't want to see a game. I just want you naked in my hotel room.*

Me: *I'm not sure I can work it around my schedule. Practice is grueling now that I'm on the starting line.*

York: *Don't give me that bullshit. I'm a big girl. Have I been replaced by a regular you have in Florida?*

Me: *Listen, I'll message you tomorrow. I just finished a game and I'm about to meet up with the guys.*

York: *Just remember what you're saying no to.*

Another picture comes up of her in a black lingerie number that barely covers anything.

Pocketing my phone, I slide into the driver's seat. "Sorry."

"No problem." Ande faces straight ahead with her hands clasped in her lap, nervous energy rolling off her.

I drive out of the parking lot, making our way to Carmelo's. It isn't far from the arena, so I don't have much time to get out what I want to say to Ande. We're both quiet until I park and turn off the ignition.

"Can I ask you a question?" I'm still unsure how to approach this subject. I've never had someone make up a boyfriend as an excuse not to date me before.

"Sure." Her voice is soft, as though she knows what I'm about to ask.

"You and Trevor..." I let the words hang there, hoping she'll pick up where I left off.

She turns in her seat to face me. "I'm sorry. I shouldn't have lied, but it was the only thing I could think of so that you wouldn't push me to date you."

Talk about a knife to the heart. Jesus. Is the idea of

dating me really that repulsive to her? I thought we had a connection when we were together on the island.

I clear my throat. "You could've just told me."

She inhales deeply. "Could I have?"

"Yes." I nod.

"And you would've just accepted that?"

I run my thumb along the stitching of the fabric on my steering wheel. "I don't make a habit of chasing women who don't want me."

"That's exactly it."

"What?" I glance at her and she's staring out the window at the sidewalk.

"I do like you, Cory. But remember when we went to the taco place, and I told you why I never called?"

I nod.

"Those reasons still exist. I'm still messed up from Michael. If we were to get involved right now, I'd punish you and be mistrusting of you because of what he did to me. Like tonight. All those women." She gestures at me.

When Ande told me about her ex-boyfriend and we decided to have a fling, I knew he'd done damage that would take time for her to get over. I also knew my lifestyle was a detriment to someone with major trust issues, and that was before I decided to live it up over the past year. But if I thought for a second Ande could be a part of my life, I never would've slept with anyone else.

"Is it that hard to believe that if you were my girlfriend, those other women would be invisible to me?"

She huffs but smiles. "I've read all the stuff about you."

"But if you'd called me or returned my phone call months ago, I never would've entertained other women. I thought you didn't want me. But if you're willing and avail-able, you're the only woman I want." I swivel in my seat and grab her hands. Her soft skin feels like silk on my calloused hands. "Do I need to explain where you stand with me?"

She shrugs. "I think I know, but I thought I did with Michael too. I thought we were going to get married and start a family. I envisioned myself as an elderly woman on a porch with him next to me, watching our grandchildren playing. And then bam, everything I thought was real wasn't. It was like I'd imagined it all. The reason I can't date you is because I know I'd be the one to destroy us. My mistrust would screw with us at every turn."

I weave our fingers together. "Then let me be a distraction."

Maybe I'll have to take baby steps with this woman, and getting back into her bed is as good a first step as any.

"What?" She narrows her eyes.

"We can do what we did on the island. Nothing serious." I shrug as if it will be easy-peasy, but the truth is, I know sleeping with her will make me want her more than I already do. But I have to keep the end goal in mind. My dad always told me nothing worth having was easy.

"Why would we do that?"

"Ande, I'll take you any way I can get you." I hold her stare for a moment.

"You're kidding, right? We just fuck and make some rules about no sleepovers or actual dates? And you're still free to screw other women?"

I shake my head. "No way. If you want to date someone else, I can't stop you, but I won't be seeing anyone but you. But as far as we go, we'd be casual."

She laughs lightly. "This is absurd."

It probably is, but if a casual relationship will help me grow closer to her and bring us to the precipice of a real relationship, I'm game.

"I'll think about it, but no promises."

I squeeze then release her hands. "Okay. Just let me know. As of right now though, you're going to go in there and party with me."

I climb out of my car and pocket my keys, rounding the front to open the passenger door for her. If all goes well, I'll have my answer tonight.

MY ONLY MISSION for the rest of the night is to show Ande a good time. I'm done with the seriousness between us. What we need is some good, old-fashioned fun. So the first thing I do when we enter Carmelo's is head to the bar and order both of us a shot.

"One. Two. Three." We each down the shot of the night, which I think is some version of a lemon drop. Definitely vodka and lemon.

I take her hand and lead her into a booth that holds Tweetie, Tedi, and Trevor.

"I thought Burrows was coming?" I ask, not seeing Kane.

"I'm sure he'll show up." Tweetie raises his hand. "A round of shots."

After we talk about the game and do another round of shots, everyone says they're not hungry, so Tweetie raises his hand again to gain our attention. "Let's go clubbing."

Ande groans. "Trevor and I have a client meeting first thing in the morning."

"One dance isn't going to kill you." Tedi climbs out of the booth over Trevor. "Let's go." Trevor slides out, and when Tweetie stands, Tedi jumps on his back. "Let's go to the karaoke bar."

"Great idea! Let's go." Tweetie points forward.

Ande tries to get Trevor's attention, but he seems into the idea, following Tweetie as if he wants to jump on his back too.

The rest of the hockey team stays behind, and a ten-minute walk later, we're at the karaoke bar. There are private rooms, so Tweetie pays our way in and, with the help of Trevor, orders pitchers of margaritas for all of us.

As we file into a room, I haven't failed to notice that Ande hasn't pulled her hand from mine yet. Tedi didn't ask any questions about Ande and Trevor while we were at Carmelo's, but I'm pretty sure she already knows.

The minute we're in the room, Tweetie searches the book and cues up his song. "Dance Monkey" by Tones & I plays.

"He does this every time." Tedi throws herself into her seat. "I'm not dancing. We have witnesses."

"Let's keep this PG. We are not having an orgy." I hold up my hands then pick up the book, bringing it over to Ande.

"Did someone say orgy? I'm in." Trevor raises his hand and laughs.

Tweetie sings, sauntering across the room toward Tedi. She's laughing and shaking her head, but we all know what's going to happen. He gets down on his knees, his hips moving from side to side. If I was jealous of any of my teammates' relationships, it might be this one. Tweetie clearly loves Tedi, and they are one-hundred-percent themselves when they're together. There're no secrets, no hiding.

Tedi finally accepts his hand, and he slides back on his knees, allowing space for her to get up and dance for him. Eventually, her hand is no longer in his, but rather her arms are raised in the air and she's circling around while her hips rotate. Tweetie gets to his feet and swings his arm around her waist, the two of them dancing together.

I remove my attention from them and focus on Ande. "Okay, do you have a song picked out yet?"

She shakes her head, flipping the pages and glancing from the book to Tedi and Tweetie and back.

When Tweetie's song is over, I stand. "Okay, I'm going up."

Tedi's on his lap and the two are practically making out. Until my song comes on. "Stuck on You" by Lionel Richie plays and Tweetie groans.

"Way too serious!" he shouts.

Trevor sits next to Ande and leans in, speaking loudly. "I guess the fake relationship's been outed or do I need to kick his ass?"

Ande laughs and shakes her head. "We're busted. Sorry. Thanks for being my fake boyfriend though."

He hits her thigh. "Anything for you. I gotta find a heartbreak song now."

Tedi points at Trevor. "I knew it. You're gay, right?"

Trevor pretends to dance by himself in the small room. "Yep."

Tweetie still looks confused, so Tedi explains to him, and his eyebrows are furrowed after she finishes.

Meanwhile, I'm on my knees in front of Ande, taking her hand in mine, but I'm not getting the action Tweetie is.

"We need to amp up this party!" Tedi says to Trevor when I'm done, and he runs over to cue up a song.

When "Dancing Queen" by ABBA comes on, Ande's hand is out of mine and she's on the floor with Trevor. I sit in the booth and watch the two of them dance together while singing. They definitely have a good friendship. Tedi springs up off Tweetie's lap to join them, and Tweetie comes to sit beside me.

"So, she lied?" he asks with a tone that makes it clear he doesn't understand.

"Yeah."

He nods. "And you still want her?"

I shrug. "Yep."

He nods again. "Okay, cool."

And that's why I love Tweetie so much. He doesn't judge, just lives his life and lets others do the same.

Then he steals the cue and puts on Elvis's "Jailhouse Rock."

By the time we leave karaoke, I feel as though I've made some progress with Ande. We had fun together and shared some laughs. The best part of the night was when Tedi and Ande sang "Rich Girl" by Gwen Stefani and Eve because Ande seemed to have released the anxiety that's plagued her since she started hanging out with us. It was as though the woman I met on vacation reappeared. I can't help but hope that woman might be willing to give me another shot.

Still, she went home with Trevor. But tomorrow's another day.

CHAPTER 9

Ande

My sunglasses are firmly in place when I walk into my office the next day.

"Hi, Ande!" I cringe and shut my eyes for a moment after Tabitha, our peppy receptionist, greets me. "The clients aren't here yet. Trevor told me to assure you the minute you walked in."

"Thanks, Tabitha," I murmur and sip my coffee, hoping it works its magic and makes this hangover disappear.

I sit in my chair and my head feels as if it weighs a thousand pounds, so I rest it on my desk for a moment.

"Knock, knock. I knew you'd be in bad shape." Trevor walks into my cubicle. Though I usually love the smell of his cologne, this morning it's making me nauseated.

"I just needed a little more sleep."

"That Tedi, she's a pusher."

I peek one eye open to find Trevor looking very presentable and not at all like he enjoyed one too many margaritas last night. There aren't even any bags under his eyes.

"How can you possibly look so good?" I pick up my head, but it falls to rest on the back of my chair.

"I switched to water midway through the night without telling Tedi so she wouldn't peer pressure me."

I wave him off. "I think the fun got out of control."

"You could say that. Now that the secret is out, I feel a lot more comfortable. Are you disappointed you went home by yourself last night?" He waggles his eyebrows.

My only response is a groan.

He laughs. "Had to fight with Cory about it. What's going on with you two now that he knows I prefer dicks over chicks?"

"Fight with him?"

He waves me off. "Nothing I can't handle. I told him soon enough he'll be the one driving you home."

My eyebrows scrunch, not understanding what he's talking about.

"So, what's going on?"

My phone beeps and I groan again, reaching down to find it somewhere in my massive purse. When I do, there are a string of messages from my sister.

"It's my sister," I tell Trevor.

Pattie: *Hey girl.*

Pattie: *Are you ignoring me?*

Pattie: *I'm coming into town this weekend but I won't see you until Saturday. I've got plans Friday. ;)*

Why can't I be more like her?

Me: *Cool. I'll be at my apartment whenever you finish with your fling.*

Pattie: *Wait til I give you the deets on this one. You'll be drooling.*

"She blowing you off again?" Trevor asks, which is a legit question.

My sister isn't known for her faithfulness to anyone but her one-night stands and guys who are as afraid of commitment as her. I often wonder how two people can be brought up in the same household and have such different viewpoints and needs. My sister and I couldn't be more different.

"Sort of? Before she comes to see me, she's going to hook up with someone."

Trevor huffs and shakes his head. "I love that she's so open and free. It's refreshing, but at the same time, she needs to nurture the platonic relationships in her life."

I smile at Trevor for being concerned about me. I told him how annoying it is to be so far down on my sister's list of priorities. Then he shared with me how his brother didn't disown him but acts as if he's not really gay. Never asks questions, and if the topic gets brought up, he's quick to change it in a different direction. So I like to think of Trevor as the brother I never had.

Me: *Can't wait. Text me when you're on your way.*

I don't bother asking how she knows someone local, because the reality is that she knows someone everywhere.

Pattie: *You got it. I could always ask if he's got a friend...*

Me: *No thanks.*

The last thing I need is yet another man to complicate my life. I have my hands full with Cory. I drop my phone back in my purse, pretending not to be annoyed or hurt by my sister.

"Back to last night. I want details. Now." Trevor lifts his wrist to glance at his watch. "I've waited long enough."

"There isn't much to tell. I told him the truth—that I'm too emotionally damaged to date a guy in his position."

Trevor chuckles and leans his ass against my desk, stretches his legs out, and crosses his ankles. "No, you're not."

"I am. Waiting for him to get past all those women last night made me realize I can barely handle a relationship with an insurance salesman, much less a professional hockey player almost every woman swoons over."

Trevor holds my gaze. "In all honesty, he seems like a great guy."

"You've seen the blogs and stuff." I sigh.

"Who says those are truthful?"

I consider what he's saying. I guess women could lie, but why would they do that? And it wasn't like Cory denied anything when I mentioned it to him. "He's proposing a relationship with no strings attached."

Trevor's eyebrows rise. "Really?"

"I think he thinks going slow is better than rushing me into a relationship. I got the distinct feeling he thinks he'll prove me wrong."

Trevor nods. "Good for him. Trick you into falling for him and having a relationship with him." He chuckles.

My office phone rings, and I answer. Tabitha tells me the client is here, and I pass the message along to Trevor.

He puts his hand on my shoulder. "Time to get pretty. Ditch the sunglasses and pep up. Try to look like you weren't flirting with a Florida Fury player all night." He winks and walks out of my cubicle.

I take off my sunglasses, squinting at the lights and the stinging they cause in my eyes. My phone dings and I groan but grab it quickly, hoping my sister isn't asking me what to wear to seduce her guy tonight.

Cory: *I don't want to rush you, but please think about my proposition today.*

I click off my phone, knowing I have a lot of thinking to do. My body screams hell yes, but putting myself out there again feels risky. It's like placing my last twenty down at the craps table, knowing I've already gambled away my rent for the month. And when it comes to gambling, the house always wins. As far as I'm concerned, I've never been the house.

AFTER THE MEETING, Trevor and I decide to head to Del Toros because I'm hoping tacos will help with my hangover. When we walk in, I'm expecting to be greeted by Juan, not Cory and Kane.

I step back. "What are you two doing here?"

"Kane said he wanted tacos after our midmorning work-out, and I told him about this place." Cory steps closer to me.

Juan approaches us after seating another table and he waves his finger to see who he should seat.

"Four." Cory puts his fingers in the air. "You don't mind, do you?" he asks us.

"Not at all," Trevor says. "Fair warning though. She's hungover and irritable."

Trevor steps up to Kane's side and they walk ahead of us. Juan seats us at a booth, which normally wouldn't bother me except Trevor is quick to slide in next to Kane, leaving me beside Cory.

"Figure the non-hockey players should each sit next to the hockey players. There's probably not enough room for all those muscles to fit on one bench." Trevor picks up his menu as if he's never been here before just to avoid my glare. We both know he's not an adventurous eater at restaurants. Once he finds what he likes, that's what he gets every time.

"Hey, Juan. Can we get a round of horchatas?" Cory circles his finger around the table. "You're gonna love it," he says to Kane.

Trevor raises his hand. "Minus one. I'll have a diet."

"Be right back." Juan leaves the table.

There's an awkward silence for a moment before Kane fills it. "So, you two work around here?"

"Just up the street," I say.

"And what do you guys do?" he asks.

"Graphic design. A lot of logos and company headers. Paper and signage," I say.

"Artsy type, eh?" He nods in approval. "I used to love to draw in high school and stuff. Once I got to the pros, I kind of fell off."

"Sounds like me and my journaling. I wrote religiously when I was a teenager, then one day I didn't write and then two and before I knew it, it'd been a long time."

"I used to love to read," Cory says.

"Really?" I shift to look at him.

"Yeah. You'd think I'd do more of it since we spend so much time traveling."

Juan delivers the drinks and we each order tacos, deciding on different kinds for Kane and Cory to try. Trevor orders the chicken ones for himself like I knew he would.

"What kind of books did you read?" I ask Cory after Juan leaves.

Cory glances at me, his full mouth over his straw, sucking up the horchata, and an ache forms in my belly. Those gorgeous lips and what they did to my body are at the forefront of my mind.

Once he swallows, a cocky grin forms on his mouth. "The Jack Reacher kind. Badass drifter comes into town and blows everyone's plans up."

"I just watched the movies," Kane says.

"Books are better," Cory and I say in unison.

He points at me with a big smile. "You read them?"

I shrug. "It was something I did with my dad before he passed. We had our own little book club of two."

"I'm sorry," Cory says, and his hand slides under the table and squeezes my knee. Sure, it's comforting, but it also sends a current of electricity up my thigh.

I shrug. "It's okay. It was years ago." Which is true, but it doesn't mean that the mention of it doesn't feel like a knife in the chest.

"Still."

Our eyes lock and I see sympathy in those dark hues that would make any woman swoon.

"How did you lose him? May I ask?" Kane interrupts us.

I clear my throat, focusing on him across the table. "Drug addiction. He was a carpenter, hurt his back, started taking pain pills, then it just spiraled from there."

I'm glad that I'm able to say that without shedding a tear. Sometimes I think we were lucky because we didn't have to deal with his drug addiction for years and years. In the end, it affected his heart.

"That shit is dangerous. I've known some players over the years who had similar stories. Got injured and it just got out of control from there. I'm sorry you lost your dad." Kane says it as though he's all too aware how much a death of a parent can change someone.

It's odd not to have the person who was your number one fan on this earth anymore. My sister deals with it by keeping everyone, including me, at a distance. But after my dad's death, I yearned to have a family again. A person who has my back no matter what.

"Thank you," I say and glance at Trevor, who is looking at me with concern.

"And your mom?" Cory asks gently.

"She left us when we were young. Never meant for motherhood, I guess. Or so she said in the note she left my dad. I think that's why I ended up reading Jack Reacher instead of *Twilight*." I chuckle, although no one else at the table does. "Anyway, where is Juan with the tacos?"

I glance around the restaurant to distract myself, but Cory's hand is on my leg again, providing me comfort.

I glance over and he opens his mouth to say something, but I speak first. "I know you're sorry. Everyone is always sorry."

It's his eyes that almost bring me to tears and break through the barrier I put around the part of myself that wants to fall apart while knowing someone is there to pick me up. Cory could be that person. But if I let myself fall apart, how do I really know he'll be there to pick up the pieces?

CHAPTER 10

"Dance with me?"
-Cory

Ande

I decided to take an Uber to Imogen and Warner's wedding dinner because I'll need to have a few drinks to calm my nerves. The happy couple eloped on a whim a couple of weekends ago during the couple of days the Fury had off, and they're hosting a dinner tonight to celebrate their nuptials.

Trevor was supposed to be my date, but he had a mysterious last-minute client dinner to attend. How convenient.

I had a group video chat with both Brit and Sophie before I came just to work up the courage to be here. It had been a while since we chatted, so I filled them in on everything going on with me. Talking to them helped. We were all on vacation together when I met Cory, so they saw firsthand how smitten I was with him. They were also insanely jealous that I was going to Warner Langley's wedding and ordered me to take lots of pictures, which I will not be doing.

Being invited was a surprise in the first place since I barely know Imogen or Warner, but they've both been so kind and welcoming to me that declining the invitation didn't feel like the right thing to do.

I walk into the event space and even the foyer is gorgeous. I would expect no less from Imogen. The place-card table has a treelike statue with flowers, crystals, and white tree branches intertwined. As if that's not enough, white twinkle lights are wrapped around it, making it a masterpiece I can barely turn away from.

"Ande!" Imogen spots me and walks away from Warner.

I catch him putting back a place card, then he smiles at us, breaking the distance. Imogen wraps her arms around me in a hug that would suggest we've known one another longer than we have, but she's that type of person.

"Congratulations. This is beautiful," I say.

"Thank you, and thank you for coming."

Warner puts one arm around me and kisses my cheek. I congratulate him and he says thank you.

"No Trevor, huh?" Imogen smooths her hands down her champagne silk dress.

I cringe. "Sorry, it was so last minute. I feel bad."

I messaged Imogen as soon as I found out Trevor wouldn't be coming, because I felt bad that they would be paying for a dinner no one would eat.

"We're hockey players, Ande, someone will eat the meal," Warner assures me, then he smiles at someone over my shoulder. "Jet."

My body tenses and Imogen giggles. The two of us share a look as if she's my best friend in junior high and my crush just walked up. Am I that transparent?

"I should go find my seat, and you have guests to greet." I slide by Imogen to the table, searching for my name.

Goose bumps scatter along my arms when I feel Cory step up to my side. I don't even need to look over to know it's him. He's the only one who has that effect on me.

"You look stunning," he says in his deep voice. "That dip in the back of your dress is making my imagination go wild."

His voice is low, so if anyone is nearby, they probably

can't hear him. Hopefully he can't hear the soft moan that rumbles up my throat.

"Thank you." I find my card and look up.

He's wearing an ivory suit sans tie with a teal button-down underneath. The top two buttons are undone, giving a glimpse of his perfect warm-brown skin. He's so beautiful. There's no other way to put it. The man is one-hundred-percent beautiful and sexy and alluring.

"Good news. We're at the same table." His finger brushes mine when he points at the table number on my card.

I look over my shoulder at Imogen, who's talking to an older couple but has her eye on me. She winks and winds her arm through Warner's.

"I think someone is playing matchmaker." I look at Cory.

If he's surprised, he doesn't show it. Instead, he offers me his arm. "Let me show you to your seat then."

I slide my arm through his, the scent of his cologne filling my senses. We walk through the sheer white drapes to the dining area where again, Imogen outdid herself.

"My God," I whisper.

"Imogen is a Jacobs. They don't do anything half-assed," Cory says as we stand in awe at the scene.

White branched trees with flowers and crystals and lights adorning them are scattered throughout the room. On each table are tall vases overfilled with flowers that cascade over the rim and down onto the table. White drapery hangs from the center of the ceiling down to the edge of the room, making it feel as though we're inside a tent. The lighting is dim and romantic. It's absolutely stunning.

"This is definitely not half-assed," I say.

A man comes by with a tray of champagne. Cory takes two flutes and hands me one. The two of us head to our table. Cory holds out a chair next to the one where he put his champagne.

"I would be a lot safer if I sat on the opposite side of you," I say.

"You forget how long my legs are. Come over here, beautiful, I promise to keep my hands to myself." The glint in his eye says he's lying, and I'd be lying if I didn't admit I want to sit next to him. Hell, a huge part of me wishes we were actually each other's date. But I'm scared.

I sit, and we both sip our champagne.

"Have you thought any more about my proposition?" he asks. Thankfully, no one else is at our table yet.

"I'm thinking about it."

He sips his champagne. "Maybe I'll convince you tonight."

My fingers tighten around my glass. "Can I ask you a question?"

"Anything." He's facing me instead of the table, his long, muscular legs parted around my chair.

"Why didn't you bring a date?"

He chuckles and shakes his head. "You really don't get it, do you?"

"Get what?"

"If I'd brought a date, she probably would've beaten my ass."

I almost choke on my champagne but manage to get it down. "Why?"

"Because I'd have spent the whole night staring at you. Wishing I was with you."

My heart flips over. He always says the right things. Which shouldn't set off an alarm in my head, but I've *never* had a guy chase me, let alone tell me everything he's feeling. It doesn't feel real.

"You're too sweet, which makes you dangerous."

His head tilts. "Why dangerous?"

"It's like you're too good to be true." Our eyes lock, and a cocky smirk forms on his lips.

"Beautiful, I could say the same about you."

For a moment, I get lost in his dark eyes with flecks of amber.

"Why am I always finding you two in a compromising position?" Tedi sits down on my other side. "Tweetie and I are taking bets, how much do you think this dinner costs?"

And just like that, I'm snapped back to reality, out of the bubble Cory encases me in with his presence.

ONCE DINNER IS OVER, Warner's voice comes over the microphone. All chatter ceases and everyone gives him their attention.

"I just wanted to thank everyone for coming and celebrating with us tonight. I know some people were disappointed we decided to elope and only include our families at the wedding, and we hope in the end you understand that I couldn't wait another second for Imogen to be my wife. As some of you know, our road here wasn't easy, and there's a lot I would change, but regardless of that, we're exactly where we were supposed to end up—together." There are a few awws and ohs in the crowd. "Now if my gorgeous wife could join me for a moment."

Imogen stands, a smile on her face that I'm not sure Mike Tyson could smack off. Warner slides his arm along her small waist and tucks her into his side. That move alone makes me yearn to have someone who cares for me that much. He hands her the microphone.

"Hi, everyone. First, thank you so much for being here this evening. Your presence means a lot. As if our wedding wasn't enough to celebrate, we have another announcement." She looks at Warner, then at her family's table. "Mom. Dad. Forgive me, but you know I love a big reveal."

"Oh fuck," Ford says loud enough for everyone to hear, which spurs a round of laughter since I'm pretty sure we all know what the announcement is.

"Be nice, Ford, you're going to be an uncle now," Imogen says, and cheers and applause erupt throughout the room.

"Just remember who was first," Ford shouts.

Lena stares blankly at Ford as though she can't believe he just said that.

Warner takes the microphone from his wife. "We're having twins." He winks at Ford.

Imogen snatches the microphone back. "No, we're not." She playfully swats Warner's stomach.

"Congratulations!" Aiden screams from our table.

"Traitor," Ford tells Aiden, and the room laughs again.

"Oh, and this was not the reason we got married," Warner says into the microphone. He puts his hand on Imogen's belly, running it up and down the nonexistent bump. "You make me so happy," he whispers, but the microphone picks it up.

Imogen stares at her husband and the father of her baby with love overflowing in her eyes. "We're going to have a great life."

"Get a room!" Ford yells.

A bunch of family members rush over to them, gushing over the news while the DJ starts the music. Talk about hashtag goals. I want a relationship like them one day.

A few minutes later, some of the people from our table go to offer their congratulations and Ford sits in one of their seats. "I guess that Costco-sized box of condoms I got them as a wedding gift isn't going to get any use." He sips his drink, which looks like scotch. We all laugh, but then a slow song comes on and he springs up. "Need to go find the wife. See you all later."

Tweetie and Tedi get up, and none of the others return to our table, heading to the dance floor instead.

Cory and I sit there in awkward silence for a bit, and I grow increasingly uncomfortable until he leans over, his breath causing a rush of shivers along my spine. "Dance with me?"

I shouldn't. The last thing I should do is press myself against Cory, but we're some of the only ones not dancing, and I don't think I can sit here in awkward silence much longer.

"Sure," I agree, knowing this is dangerous territory.

The minute his hand slides into mine and my stomach flips and flops like a fish out of water, I know I'm in deep, deep trouble. When we reach the dance floor, he pulls me into him and my hand touches his bicep. It's hard under my palm and my breasts suddenly feel heavy. His one hand stays in mine, while his other hand lands at the top of my ass. We sway for a moment, gaining our rhythm before he dances me around the floor as if we're on a TV show.

"Did you do *Dancing with the Stars*?" I ask.

He chuckles. "No, just living room lessons with my mom. She was adamant that I learn to dance. She and my dad are one of those cheesy couples who dance at night." He turns us in the other direction. This is so much better than slowly rotating in a circle. "I remember waking up after they'd put me to bed when I was young and sitting on the stairs, looking through the railing at them."

"That's a great memory." I smile at him.

He nods. "They love each other so much it makes me envious. Not a lot of people find their one and only." He draws back from me. "I don't remember if I told you this already, but I'm biracial. My mom is white, and my dad is Black. So they went through a lot of shit to be together." He looks around the room. "When I see something like this, with two families coming together, I often think of my parents. Not everyone was understanding of their love." He shakes his head. "Maybe that's why their love runs so deep. They had to believe in their love and fight for it."

I stare up into his eyes as a shy smile forms on his face. "I'd love to hear their love story someday."

He chuckles. "My mom would love to share it with you. She tells everyone how my dad just swept her off her feet."

I don't say it, but I think like father, like son. I feel my heart lifting out of my chest, fluttering on delicate wings into Cory's hands.

Chapter 11

"Have a seat."
—Cory

Cory

I've gotten so used to Ande being in the stands when I play that when I head out for warm-ups, it's weird not to see her there. When I asked her at the wedding to attend this game, she wasn't very forthcoming on why she couldn't, but when I texted Trevor he was more than willing to take the tickets and he's brought a guy I guess he's casual with. I put them up with the wives and girlfriends because Trevor says it's more fun up there.

Ford skates up beside me. "You look like your balloon just floated away."

"I'm just catching my breath."

"Bullshit. It's the girl. It's always the girl. Right, Warner?"

Warner skates over to us as some of the others practice hitting pucks into the goal. "Always. Amazing how they can change our moods on a dime. I'll wake up happy as shit and then Imogen will be like, 'I promised my parents we'd go over for brunch' when in reality I had plans of fucking her all day."

"Jesus, Langley, I cannot unhear those words. Stop talking about all the shit you're doing to my sister."

Warner shakes his head with a huge grin. "Okay, we sit around the fire and read the Bible, fully clothed, every night.

84

That's how we're having a baby. Immaculate conception." He skates away with the puck, leaving me with Ford.

"Why isn't Ande here?" he asks.

"Not sure, but we're just friends anyway. Not like she *has* to come."

"Tweetie said things were heating up at karaoke the other night. And I saw you guys on the dance floor at the wedding dinner." He waggles his eyebrows.

Of course, Tweetie hears Ford and finds his way over to us. "You were all over each other," he says. "Tedi is really pushing for you two. She likes Ande."

I nod, not wanting to get into the conversation since Ande can't seem to trust me enough to give me a shot.

"The only question is..." Ford pauses for dramatic effect. "Can you get rid of the puck bunnies?"

I groan and use the puck coming toward me as a way to distract myself from this conversation. I hate that they think I'm all about the bunnies, but I can't take back what I've done this year. Even if it was just the result of a bruised ego from Ande's rebuff.

When I make my way back to them, they're talking shit about their days before they were off the market.

"It's okay, it was just an honest question." Ford shrugs. "I wasn't judging. I have no right to, given my past. I was a playboy for a long ass time before Lena set me straight."

"Then?" I raise an eyebrow.

"I couldn't stand the thought of her with anyone else. I'd go mad just thinking about it, so I was smart enough to know that was my cue to take myself off the market and commit to the best woman I've ever known." He looks up at the stands. Lena's got Annabelle with her tonight and they both wave at Ford. "What a fucking fantastic life, right?"

He waves at them and skates away, going around the

back of the net to hit a goal in the other side. I watch as he skates over to the glass partition and Lena walks down the stairs. Ford takes off his glove and puts his hand on the glass and Annabelle does the same. He blows her a kiss then skates back to us.

Yeah, I want that life too. I don't want to fuck around with random women who don't give a shit about me. It wasn't even all that fun while it lasted. I want a meaningful relationship, but Ande doesn't trust me enough yet to give it a shot, which is a whole other problem.

"We can all see it, Jet." Tweetie pats me on the back. "You're not the fuck around type, but I hope you enjoyed it while you pretended to be."

I sigh. "Any advice on how to get a stage-one clinger off your back?"

I hate to ask, but York won't take no for an answer. I've been dodging her all week and she just texted me her hotel room for after the game before I got on the ice. The fact that she can't sit through the game says exactly what I need to know about her.

"Oh shit, you got a stalker?" Tweetie laughs. "Jet's got a stalker!" He skates away to take a warm-up shot.

A few of the guys laugh and wish me good luck, but none of them offer me any advice. I want to end this, but I don't want to make an enemy. I heard one guy from Seattle last year got thrown to the wolves by his regular hookup when he tried to end it. She was posting everything from he had a small dick to he gets scared during thunderstorms. It was all petty shit, but who wants to deal with that?

"Can we please stop gossiping like a bunch of high school girls!" Coach yells at us.

We straighten out in line and get serious. Well, some of

us. Ford is still joking around, and Warner joins in with him. It's now hard to remember the days they hated each other.

WE LOST THE GAME TONIGHT, and Coach isn't happy. He blames it on all the chitchat during warm-ups and said we need to start acting like professional hockey players.

On the way out of the arena, Kane clasps me on the shoulder. "Advice on the stalker. Public place and stick to the topic of being done. Don't let her sway you. Hands in pockets at all times."

I nod. Kane's probably got the sagest advice of any of my teammates. "Thanks, man."

Just then, Jana turns the corner, walking toward us. "Rumor has it you're trying to get rid of a clinger. Not sure Kane's the best guy to give you advice on that subject." Jana walks by us toward the locker room.

Kane stops and I follow suit. He turns to watch her walk away down the hall. "Jana could. She's not interested in involving feelings in a fuck."

Jana stops but doesn't turn around. I watch her inhale and exhale a deep breath, and I wait for her to stomp back over and pin Kane to the wall. The woman is kinda scary. She holds a lot of power here, and the rumors keep increasing that she's going to be taking over for her dad soon.

"You're not worth my time, Kane Burrows." She steps toward the locker room. "Watch those goals coming in from the right next game."

Man, she hits where it hurts. I raise my eyebrows at Kane.

"Watch out for those sticks, Jana. If another one gets

stuck up your ass, you might not be able to walk in those fancy heels anymore." Kane grins even though her back is to us.

She opens the door to the locker room and goes in without a word or a look behind.

"I swear, that woman." Kane shakes his head and seethes, but I catch the small grin he's trying to hide. It's like he gets off on their verbal foreplay.

We walk outside, and as always, there are women barely dressed and asking for selfies and autographs, though it's clear they really want more. I sign a few things and take a few pictures, but I don't get to everyone, instead heading to my car. A few other guys take the opportunity to soak up the attention, but I take a seat in my car and pull out my phone.

Me: *Can you meet me at the restaurant in your hotel in fifteen?*

It's probably not the best idea to meet her at the hotel, but I don't want to go anywhere we'd have to have a full meal.

York: *Why?*

Me: *I'm starved*

York: *And I'm ready to be devoured.*

Me: *I need a steak or something.*

York: *Just go eat and then come to my room.*

Me: *I don't want to eat by myself. Please... just meet me down there.*

York: **A toddler throwing a tantrum GIF**

Good to see we're going to be mature about this.

Me: *Come on, I need to eat to keep up my stamina tonight.*

I hate lying. My mom would slap me on the back of the head if she was here right now. But it's the only way I'm getting York down to the restaurant and not meeting her in her room.

York: *Finnnneeee. See you there.*

Me: *Thanks*

I toss my phone in the console and peel out of the parking lot. It only takes me five minutes to get to York's hotel. I valet my car with the restaurant and not the hotel because I have no plans of staying, no matter how big York's seduction game is.

I'm not seated at the table longer than five minutes when she saunters in, searching the room for me. She has blonde hair and a great body and her entire being screams good time. When I first met her at a Denver club, she wasn't shy to approach, which helped her get me because I was still unsure how this whole thing worked and felt weird sleeping with someone I wouldn't want anything to do with the next day. She surprised me when she texted me after we flew out. I've had a password on my phone ever since then.

"You look great." She bends down and I kiss her cheek, refusing her my lips. "Though I prefer you in less."

"Have a seat."

She pretends to pout, but she does as I ask. A waitress

comes over and we both order drinks. Me, a club soda with a lime, and her, a glass of white wine.

"Listen, York," I say, but feel her foot moving between my thighs, dangerously close to my balls. I put my hand between my legs to stop her.

"You're way too serious. I saw that you lost. Let me soothe that ego of yours." She tries to free her foot from my grip, but I refuse.

"Stop. I'm trying to tell you I'm not interested in doing this anymore."

She shifts back in the booth and her leg retreats. Thank fuck. "What?"

"There's someone I'm interested in. She's recently come back into my life, and I want to pursue what I have with her. I'm sorry."

"Why wouldn't you tell me this before I came all the way down here?"

I lean back in my seat. "I thought you had to come to Florida anyway?"

She blows out a breath. "I was coming to visit my sister, but it was to see you too."

"Then I'm sorry. I thought I was merely a pit stop while you were in town."

The waitress interrupts and brings our drinks, asking if we want anything to eat.

"No, this will be all. Can I have the check?" I ask with what sounds a lot like desperation in my voice.

York scoffs and shakes her head before taking a huge gulp of her wine. "You can't be serious? This girl doesn't even have to know about me. I can be discreet."

I want to tell her to have more self-respect, but I can't deny that I reaped the benefits of her thinking when we first met. "No, I'm not going to do that. I hope one day you'll understand, but she's special to me. I can see a future with her."

The waitress brings the check and I dig into the breast pocket of my suit jacket for my wallet, opening it to get cash out.

York lets out a low chuckle. "You're a fool. There's no such thing as happily ever after. Your teammates might think so since they're all getting married and having babies or whatever, but one day you'll all find out the truth, just like my dad did."

I say nothing and she continues.

"People are selfish, Cory, and the sooner you realize that, the sooner you'll realize you need to be selfish too."

I slide out of the booth and throw some cash on the table. "I'm sorry that's how you feel, York, but I don't believe that. Take care of yourself."

I walk out of the restaurant and hand the valet my ticket. All I want to do is message Ande and ask if I can come over, but she was clear when we parted ways at the wedding that she wanted time to think it over, so I'll give her the weekend.

Even if it kills me.

CHAPTER 12

"I need out. Now!"
—Andie

Andie

I roll over in bed and get comfortable again, ignoring the spill of light seeping through the cracks of my drapes. My bed is comfortable, and I take full advantage, sprawled out from corner to corner.

I'm drifting back to sleep when my doorbell begins ringing nonstop. Annoyance lashes me like a whip. My sister isn't supposed to be here until lunch and it's only nine o'clock in the morning. I pick up my phone and look at my Ring. My sister's chipper face fills the entire camera space.

"I brought drinks!" Pattie holds up a drink container with two coffees. "And treats!"

A white bag that looks as if it came from the bakery down the street is in her other hand. I'm hoping my favorite chocolate croissant is in that bag, although she has no idea what I like from that bakery since this is her first time visiting me since I moved.

I groan and get out of bed, throwing on a cardigan and heading to the front door. My house isn't big, but it's five blocks from the water, which was most important to me. It's quaint and unique. Two words that tell you I couldn't afford a remodel or brand-new house. But I love my built-in bookcases and the articulated carved trim that gives it character. The best thing about this place is my backyard has complete privacy from my neighbors and a water fountain that drowns out a little bit of the neighborhood noise.

I open my door and my sister barrels in, greeting me with a half hug. "It's so great to see you."

"I thought we were having lunch. I had this whole idea of packing up something and heading to the beach."

"Sand?" she says, her nose crinkling as if that's the most disgusting thing she's heard of. "How about we eat by the pool instead?"

"I don't have a pool."

"You don't?" She puts the coffees on the small kitchen counter and picks up hers. "I thought everyone in Florida had a pool?"

"Well, not me." I grab the coffee from the drink holder and peek into the bag.

Muffins.

Disappointment washes over me because I had high hopes for that chocolate croissant. Tomorrow is another day. I could wake up early and head down there. Surprise her. That's what her visit is about for me anyway—sharing with her my favorite things about Florida, including the best chocolate croissant I've ever eaten.

"This place is cute," Pattie says, still examining the space.

"Thanks." I sit in the big armchair I found on clearance. Trevor's friend, Gregg, helped me reupholster it. "Sit down. You're making me nervous."

"Why would I make you nervous? Did you see I brought you muffins?"

"I saw. Thank you."

She picks up the bag and puts it in my lap. "Have some."

I pull one out of the bag. "And why aren't you having one?"

"Oh, I ate at the hotel." She gives me that expression that says she didn't eat anything food related for breakfast.

"All the more reason you should have a muffin. You must be tired."

Do I judge my sister? Maybe a little. But only because I think she sleeps with different men all the time because of our parents. Our mom leaving, my dad loving my mom until the day he died. Pattie saw the pain he went through, and she'd rather avoid that by never getting close to someone.

"Coffee is enough for me." She raises her cup.

"Why are you here so early?" I ask, then take a sip of my coffee.

"My hookup had somewhere to be this morning, so I figured why sleep in after he said a naked goodbye to me this morning?" Her expression is one of love, but I know she's not in love with whoever this man is.

"Any hope of things getting more serious with you two?"

Pattie scoffs. "No way."

Cory and his proposition to keep things casual come to mind. I know his real hope is that things would progress with us, but I'm not my sister. If I could be with Cory without involving my heart, that wouldn't sound so bad. But I'm better off being single until I can find a guy who's safe and doesn't have a career like Cory's. One I don't think will hurt me. But I keep all that to myself because I'm not ready to talk about it yet.

I peel the wrapping from around the muffin because my stomach is growling, then put the bag on my coffee table in case my sister changes her mind and wants one. There's silence for a long time before she pretends like there hasn't been, acting excited.

"So I have to tell you about this guy from last night." She places her hand on her heart and sighs.

"You had a good time?" I ask, not really interested in the details.

"He was big and definitely knew how to use it." She wiggles in her seat. "I'm kind of sore, actually."

"Well, it's been months since I've had sex, so I wouldn't know the feeling."

"God, Ande, that's so sad. Oh, I forgot I had something to tell you."

My forehead wrinkles. "What?"

"I saw Michael. I was in Salt Lake City for business, and we were at the same hotel restaurant. How crazy is that?"

I prepare myself for her to tell me she slept with my ex. "Did you..."

Her smile loses its luster, and she stares blankly at me. "Seriously, Ande?"

I shrug. "You and hotel usually equals you sleeping with someone."

"Jeez, judge much?" She gets up from the couch and walks around the space, examining every knickknack. I wait for her to pick on me for something.

"Well?"

She whips around from my bookcase. "No. Actually, I was trying to break this a lot more delicately, but he's married and expecting a kid."

The breath I was already holding remains lodged in my throat as her words rerun through my head. "Married? Kid?"

"Yep." She sits back down, showing no regret for her harsh delivery. "He looked super happy. Told me to tell you hello."

I nod. "Nice. Well, hopefully for her sake, he can keep it in his pants."

I'm not upset my ex is moving on with his life. Well, I am. But not because I want it to be me doing those things with him. I want to find my own someone to do those things with.

And as we sit in silence for a moment, I'm reminded why my sister and I haven't ever been that close. We're too different. She's petty and selfish and retaliates with a vengeance when she thinks someone has wronged her. I would never deliver news I thought would hurt her like that.

"Aren't you over him yet? Jeez, Ande, it's been like a year."

"Try eight months."

She laughs and rolls her eyes.

At this point, I want to change the subject. "You know what, Trevor was telling me about a club we should go to tonight. Why don't I ask him if he wants to join us?" I get up to retrieve my phone from the bedroom.

"Is that your gay boss? You know, you amaze me, Candy Ande. You're hung up on an ex who treated you wrong, then you go and hang around men who won't ever have an interest in you." She shakes her head. "I wish you'd just live like me for one night. You wouldn't judge when you're screaming in bliss."

I smile. "Let me go call Trevor." I snag the bag of muffins and retreat to my bedroom.

LUCKY FOR ME, I have a friend like Trevor, who is willing to run interference between my sister and me. The three of us, along with Trevor's new guy, Gregg, wait in line outside the club. Pattie is flirting with the bouncer, and surprisingly, it's not working for her.

"Believe me, we've tried. No one skips the line except

superstars and athletes." Trevor puts his hand on her shoulder.

"I could've used my connection," she mumbles, and I ignore her. I'm not into listening to her brag about her conquests at the moment.

Finally, some people leave the club—or maybe they were kicked out, I'm not sure. They don't seem happy to leave, but them leaving means me going in, so I'm thrilled. We file into the club and it's smaller than I thought, but I guess that's why it's elite.

Right away, Trevor has shots from the bar and he's swindling his way into a booth a group of people are leaving. The dance floor is packed and I'm already dancing in my seat. I really hope tonight is a good night. I want Pattie and me to have fun together.

"To York, welcome to Florida," I say, and we all clang our shot glasses together before tipping them back.

"I thought your name was Pattie," Gregg shouts over the music.

I laugh. "That's just my nickname for her. Her nickname for me is Candy Ande." I raise my eyebrows, waiting for him to put two and two together. Which never happens.

Trevor swoops in and saves the day. "Ande, the little mint chocolate candies, and York, the peppermint patties? They're named after candy."

Gregg's mouth opens and his eyes widen. "Oh, I wish I would've thought of that. Brilliant. Your parents were brilliant."

"Actually, they were drug addicts and abandoners, but thanks." York hops down from the booth, dancing in front of us. "Come on!"

"Just go." I wave her off and that's all she needed to head out to the dance floor by herself.

"Should one of us...?" Gregg asks right before she disappears.

"No. She'll be fine. Probably won't even come home with me tonight."

Gregg gives me a look of sympathy and runs his hand down my arm. "I guess that's why you don't choose your family, but you choose your friends."

Trevor puts his arm around my shoulders and kisses my temple. "Damn right."

For the rest of the night, we drink and dance. York is always a few people away, never really interacting with the three of us, but I can tell she's got her eye on some guy who seems to be floating between her and another woman on the dance floor.

Trevor has a constant stream of drinks flowing, and we basically only see York when she comes to grab one. I have so much fun it isn't until we decide to go home and leave the bar that the lack of lasers and booming bass alert me to how drunk I am.

I stumble on the sidewalk and Gregg comes to my side, holding me up. "Your carriage just turned into a pumpkin, darling."

"Let's get these two home." Trevor helps York, who is coming home with me, much to my surprise. Then again, it wasn't for lack of trying on her part. "Then we can go back to my place."

"To fuck? You're going to fuck, aren't you?" I get into the back seat of the waiting Uber. "I need to get fucked. Do you know how long it's been? So long, and of course the last guy I had it with was just the best. He ruined me. He screwed hard, but then he could be really soft too. I don't think I ever came so much in a week in my life." As the words leave my mouth, I already know I'm going to regret them when I'm sober, but I can't seem to stop myself.

My head hits the headrest and I close my eyes, remembering what it was like to be with Cory. Maybe I should call him for a booty call.

"Who is this guy with the magical dick?" York asks.

"Just this guy who wants to be with me, but he's scary."

"Scary?" York asks, slurring a bit.

"She means emotionally scary. He's a great guy." Trevor leans forward and looks at my sister. "Too bad you weren't in town yesterday. Ande could've gotten you tickets to the game."

I close my eyes from the nausea rolling around my stomach.

"What game?" York elbows me in the ribs and I want to tell her to back off, but it feels like too much effort right now.

"The Florida Fury hockey game. We went last night." Gregg turns around in the front seat. "Talk about having sweet dreams after a night of watching all those guys and the testosterone they're throwing around." He fans himself, and I laugh.

"You follow Florida Fury hockey?" York asks me, sounding almost skeptical.

I shrug. "I know someone who plays for them."

Her eyes widen. "You know one of the players?" She says it almost like she can't believe it.

I straighten up in my seat, ready to accept the challenge in her voice. "Yeah, I do."

"How did you meet him?"

Trevor cuts in. "It's the perfect meet-cute. Vacation fling. They met at a resort and slept together all week. Then she gets transferred here and she doesn't look him up but ends up running into him at the supermarket. Then somehow we got invited to a barbeque and we got to see Warner Langley propose to Imogen Jacobs. So wild, I swear."

"Which player?" York completely disregards Trevor's story, her eyes narrowed on me.

I narrow my eyes right back. "Why do you care?"

"The guy I was with last night is a Fury player," she says slowly.

I wave her off. "No way."

"Yes way."

"Who then?"

"Cory Freeman. The new center."

I freeze, then slap my hand hard on the window. "I need out. *Now!*"

The Uber driver stops, and I open the door, rush out, and throw up on the sidewalk. This cannot be happening.

I knew Cory was too good to be true.

CHAPTER 13

"Just send it!"

Andie

"**D**o you want us to stay?" Trevor asks when the Uber stops outside my house.

I shake my head. "No. You guys go enjoy the rest of your night."

York didn't stop asking me questions when I got back in the car, but I didn't want to answer her with some random Uber driver present. Finally, Trevor told her to stop and wait until we got home. So now she's on my porch with her hand on her hip.

"Well, call me if you need me. I'll check on you tomorrow." He kisses my cheek and heads back to the car.

I retrieve my keys and unlock my front door. Even throwing up and the news of Cory sleeping with my sister hasn't sobered me up completely. All I want to do is go to bed and wake up to a time before I ever met Cory.

"Now can we talk?" York follows me into my living room, beelining right to my liquor cabinet.

"What do you want to talk about? The fact we've slept with the same guy? Or the fact that said guy has been pursuing me hard since we reconnected here and now I find out about this?" I lie down on the couch.

"It's you," she says in disgust.

"What's me?"

"Nothing. I need another drink and I think you do too." She brings over two shot glasses and a bottle of vodka.

"If we're doing a shot, can we at least flavor it?" I ask.

"You have slim pickings here." She pours two shots and I sit up on my couch, accepting one of them. "When is the last time you slept with him?"

"Not last night." I down the shot. "And you know what? I was actually starting to believe his bullshit. That he'd changed. That I was someone special to him."

York flips off her heels and sits cross-legged on the chair. "Men are pigs. See why I don't let feelings get involved?"

"Definitely." Anger makes my cheeks heat.

She pours another two shots and I down the second one without waiting to clink my glass with hers.

"Slow down, you've already thrown up." She tilts her head back and gulps down her shot.

"That was because I found out we've slept with the same man!" I stand and grab my computer, pulling up images of Cory. Turning the screen to her, I ask with the hopes we're wrong, "This is him? The guy you slept with last night?"

She nods and tips the bottle to fill another round of shots. I let that one sit there because pretty soon I'm going to pass out and I'm way too angry to pass out.

"Argh!" My hands fist at my sides. I want to punch something. Preferably Cory's stupid face. I push the computer away. "I want to call him up right now and scream and yell and shame him for making me think he was a different kind of guy."

"It won't do any good. That's just the way guys are. I'm not sure why you think differently all the time." York almost looks smug.

I'm starting to think her way of living is way better than

mine. She's not having her heart ripped out and broken time and time again.

"I want to get back at him." I lean back on the couch. "Make him feel like I do."

I rest my head on the back of the couch cushion and close my eyes. Disbelief still courses through my veins, but I can't stay in the dark any longer.

Cory Freeman is a player.

He played me on vacation and he's playing me now. And that idiot doesn't even know he slept with my sister last night. Probably thinks I'm still considering his stupid offer!

"You said he's been coming on to you hard lately?" York asks, pulling me from my thoughts.

I open my eyes, pick up the shot glass, and take the last one. "Yeah. Jackass."

"Tell me about the vacation fling?"

I spill the entire story to York. From meeting on the bus ride to the resort to the last day. How I slept with him and how the day he left the resort, I got offered a job here. That I thought it was creepy to contact him and doubled down on that when I saw all the action he was getting. Then how we ran into each other at the grocery store, the whole pretending Trevor was my boyfriend thing, and Cory calling me out once he figured out it was a lie. Lastly, I tell her about the conversations I've had with him lately. How I thought I might put myself out there and give the casual relationship he offered a try.

Her eyes light up at that part.

"What?"

"That's what you're going to do. You're going to lead him on, make him fall for you, and break his heart."

How did I not think of that? He can get a taste of his own medicine.

But my excitement quickly fades. I don't go around and purposely hurt people. "That's not me."

"For once, do something for yourself, Ande. He totally played you and deserves it."

"But what if I fall for him?" I voice my biggest fear.

She laughs. "I can see where that's a concern of yours. I'll make sure you don't."

I bite my lip and she pours another two shots, lifting her glass up to me.

"Let's give him exactly what he gave us."

I pick up my glass and clink it with hers, downing more vodka and agreeing to deceive Cory. York is right. He didn't think anything of playing me, so why not dick around with his emotions and see how he feels about it?

"Now, one last thing." York picks up my phone and hands it to me. "Text him that you're all in."

I grab my phone and pull up his contact. I type out the sentence and my thumb hovers over the send button.

"Just send it!" York says.

I press down on the screen and off goes the message.

No turning back now.

CHAPTER 14

Cory

I'm midworkout, unable to stop smiling, when Kane and Warner walk into the gym.

"What's got you so fucking happy, eh?" Kane asks, stripping off his sweatshirt.

Warner stretches. "You'd think your fairy godmother just came to visit."

Kane stares at Warner with scrunched-up eyebrows. "What?"

Warner shakes his head. "Fuck, man, Gen's got me all messed up. We got in this big argument the other day about how Annabelle doesn't need a fairy godmother to get what she wants. She can go after it just like every man in this world does. Suddenly, Gen's telling me that she doesn't wear heels for me, she wears them for herself." He runs his hand through his hair, clearly stressed. "I know she was torturing me with those heels on purpose before we got back together, man."

Kane glances in my direction. "Is this real? Couples argue about shit like this?"

Leave it to Kane. Sometimes I wonder if he'll ever find a woman to settle down with. He's a veteran in the league, stuck in his ways, and clearly not going to entertain his wife dictating how he can talk to his daughter.

"Unfortunately, yes. If by chance our baby is a girl, I'll treat her like a princess. But sure as shit, she'll be on skates as soon as she's walking. She'll be going to spas with Imogen and playing hockey with me."

I situate myself under the bar and motion Kane over to spot me.

"Enough about me, what's up with you, Jet?" Warner stares at me while Kane heads to the top of the bench.

"Ande's finally agreed to see me. Got a text last night that she wants to give a casual relationship a try." I push up the bar and lower it back down, but I don't miss the look exchanged between the two of them.

"I thought you wanted to get serious with her?" Warner asks.

"I do. But this is all she's willing to agree to right now." I grunt as I lift the bar again.

"Is she close to Jana by chance?" Kane deadpans.

I crinkle my forehead. "No."

Warner waves. "That would be my wife she's becoming besties with."

"No shit. I meant it as a joke," Kane says.

"Then laugh." Warner raises an eyebrow.

Meanwhile, I'm breathing out harshly with every rep and my arms grow tired.

"I don't laugh at my own jokes."

"Why not?" I ask.

"Because that's lame." He looks at me. "Two more, Jet."

"Then you need to change your inflection. You're all monotone, and what the hell is going on with you and Jana anyway?" Warner changes the subject.

I'd be lying if I said I'm not intrigued as well. Supposedly the guy hates the woman, but anyone can see the way Kane looks at her.

"Nothing is going on with us."

Warner nods. "Okay then. Jet, don't tell him shit until he decides to open up to us." Warner sits on the bench next to us.

"What are you, five?" Kane shakes his head.

I push up my last rep and Kane helps me get the bar back in place before I sit up and grab a towel. "What's going down?"

Kane blows out a breath and waves for me to get up off the bench. I do and he lies down in my place, Warner standing to spot him. "There isn't anything going on. She's the owner's daughter. No way can she get involved with a player. Even if that player might retire this year."

"What?" Warner asks, looking at me with disbelief.

Kane is older for the league, but he's still got great performance on the ice.

"Come on, guys, don't act like you don't notice it. I'm off. Just a bit, but off."

"No, I haven't noticed. You saved thirty-five shots last game," Warner says.

"And let in three." His voice is filled with disgust.

"It's not like we're making playoffs anyway," I grumble.

"I haven't said anything to anyone. I'm still mulling it over." Kane finishes his reps and sits up. "Nothing's final, so don't mention this to anyone." He gives Warner a stern glare because we all know he shares everything with Imogen.

He's quick to hold up his hands. "I promise, man, but retirement? You're too young."

Kane snickers. "You only think that because you're not too far off from me."

Which is probably the truth. I can't imagine not playing this game. Every time I'm on the ice is a pinch-me-I'm-dreaming moment. But too soon, you're not the young guy anymore. Soon you're injured more than healthy. Soon you're warming the bench with the rookies. And that's a hard pill for any athlete to swallow.

I get where Warner's head's at. He's not old by any means, but he's on the walkway to the door while Kane is already knocking on the door. I wonder how I'll handle that when the time comes.

"Enough about this depressing shit, tell us where you're taking Ande for your first date?" Warner lowers himself onto the bench.

"You know it's gotta be big," Kane says, sitting on the other bench while I spot Warner. "She's finally given you a chance. Now you have to prove you're worth it."

I shrug. "I just want to be alone with her."

"Okay, rookie, one piece of advice—do not try to sleep with her the first time you guys go out together." Kane wipes his face.

"I wasn't going to try to sleep with her tonight, but I don't want to be in a crowded restaurant where people might recognize me."

"Listen to this superstar," Warner says, laughing as he pushes up another rep.

"But I don't wanna go to a movie and not be able to talk either." I ignore Warner's comment.

Warner finishes his reps and sits up to rest. "I can ask for reinforcements." What he means is he can ask Imogen, but I want it to be my idea.

"That's okay, man, I'll think of something."

"That's over now. Let's work the fuck out now and stop talking about women." Kane moves over to the barbells in front of the mirror.

Warner joins him while I rack my brain on what Ande might want to do for our first official date.

After my workout and shower, I sit on my couch back home and dial up Ande.

She answers on the fourth ring. "Hey."

"Hey."

There's a beat of silence.

"So, I got your text…"

"I figured." Something's off in her voice. Maybe she's as nervous as me. I know this is a big step for her to trust me.

"I wanted to see when you're available. Unfortunately, we couldn't have picked a worse week. I have away games, and I won't be home until late Friday."

"Oh." She's quiet. "That's okay."

"I wish I could pack you up in my suitcase."

She laughs, but it's not a genuine laugh. Not the same one from our time in paradise. My heart is practically beating out of my chest. Did she change her mind about us already?

"How about next Saturday? It's a rare weekend when I don't have a game." I squeeze my eyes shut, waiting for her response.

"Sure."

"Unless…"

"What?"

"I know today's Sunday and all, but would you want to go grab a bite to eat and maybe walk on the beach? Just something so we can see each other?"

There's another long silence and I hold my breath for a beat.

"I really want to see you."

"I have work to catch up on," she says, then there's a muffled sound like her hand is over the receiver.

"Ande?"

"Yeah, I'm here. Sorry, my sister is in town." Again there's a muffled sound.

"Oh sorry, I didn't know. No worries, we can plan something for next weekend."

"No, it's okay. She's leaving in an hour to catch a flight home, so how about four?"

Thank fuck. For a moment, I thought that text was some kind of prank on her part, or she was so wasted last night she regretted sending it.

"Four is great. Can you send me your address?"

Again with the silence. What's going on with her?

"Can we meet somewhere?" she asks.

"You don't want me to have your address? Ande, I'm not a stranger. You know my damn dick size."

And that comment brings back memories of our time in the tropics. How soft her skin was. How shy she was at first. How damn good she felt to wake up next to in the morning.

"Cory!"

"Sorry. I just meant…" I realize she's just being cautious, and I can't blame her for that. I know she wants to take it slow. "I understand. Let's meet at the Riverwalk."

"Okay. Four at the Riverwalk. See you then."

"Ande?" I say before she can hang up.

"Yeah?"

"Thanks for trusting me." I hope she knows I don't take it lightly that she's placing her trust in me. I won't disappoint her.

"Sure. No problem."

What? My forehead wrinkles.

"Bye, Cory."

She hangs up, and I sit there for a moment, trying to make sense of our conversation. Maybe she's one of those people who aren't comfortable on the phone. Or maybe she's so scared she's not being herself.

I cross my fingers that she's back to her usual self tonight.

Then I grab my laptop from the coffee table. Time to do some research on how to make this the best date Ande's ever been on.

CHAPTER 15

Andie

I've been second-guessing this plan since I texted Cory. York assures me we're doing the right thing, that it's about time one of these assholes who thinks it's okay to break hearts gets what's coming to them, but I'm not her. I can't hide my feelings as well as she does. And I'm still really pissed at Cory. That he'd act like he wants a relationship with me and sleep with my sister is like a dagger in the chest. I'm not sure I'll be able to keep from saying something.

I walk down the Riverwalk, seeking Cory, but other than some families and couples, there aren't any guys lingering around. Then I turn a corner and find him sitting on a park bench, his ankle resting on his knee, an arm stretched along the back of the bench. He has sunglasses and a hat on, which I'm guessing is to disguise himself. He looks as gorgeous as he always does, and for a moment, I forget all about York.

When he turns in my direction and his smile widens, it all rushes back and so does the bile rising up my throat. *He slept with my sister on Friday night.* My hand instinctively goes to my stomach.

Then he stands and his height is so dominating that a few people glance in his direction, probably wondering if they know him. He's been the face of the Fury for the last couple weeks and I'm sure that's come with a lot more recognition with the public.

"Hey, beautiful," he says.

All I envision for a moment is him saying that to York. Naked in bed when they woke up after a night full of sex just yesterday morning.

The fact that he unknowingly slept with my sister months ago doesn't bother me as much. Maybe it should, but we weren't even talking back then, and I know my sister. It meant nothing to her, and if she'd thought it would mean something to Cory, she wouldn't have slept with him to begin with. But the fact that he slept with her again when he was telling me how much he cared about me makes me want to throw up all over his Air Jordans.

I force a smile. "Hey."

"I figure we'd walk for a while, maybe stop by a bar or two. Get some appetizers and drinks."

"Sure."

We walk, but we're not fifty feet before a man with deep-umber skin and who I assume is his son comes up to us.

"Sorry to interrupt. Sorry, ma'am," the dad says to me. "We're huge fans. Would you mind?" He nods beside him at his son.

The kid is looking at Cory with wide eyes but no smile, holding out a marker and a piece of paper.

"Sure." Cory accepts the marker and piece of paper, signing his name. "What's your name, buddy?" He crouches down to the kid's level.

"Justin," he says almost inaudibly.

"Do you play hockey, Justin?" Cory asks.

Justin nods.

"He plays street hockey mostly. But he just joined an ice

hockey team." His dad squeezes his shoulder. "He loves watching you play. That stretch you skated last week against Nashville was insanely fast."

Cory looks at the dad and smiles. "Thanks. You want to know how I got so fast?" he says to Justin.

A few people walk by and watch the scene unfolding. Some pull out their phones—most likely to try to figure out who Cory is. I really hope this doesn't turn into a full-on mob of people asking for autographs. The fact these two recognized him amazes me.

"How?" Justin asks.

"I ate all my vegetables, and I practiced every day. But most of all, I just had fun. If you don't love it, don't do it. But if you love it, give it your all. That was my mom's motto when I was growing up."

Justin's dark eyes sparkle, and he smiles. "I eat my broccoli and I love street hockey. Ice hockey is harder with the pads."

Cory nods. "Yeah, but as you grow, you'll get used to it. Do you have fun on the ice?"

"Well, I can't go as fast, and it's cold, but yeah." The young boy nods.

"Then keep working at it. I fell in love with hockey the first time I was on the ice, but that's not true for everybody. Some kids grow into it."

He bumps knuckles with the boy and stands, stretching to his full height and making him tower over the dad.

"I can't thank you enough. You know, there aren't a lot of Black hockey players out there. When I suggested Justin play hockey, he told me it was a white man's sport. Then you got drafted to the Fury, so I took him to a game. It made a real difference for him to see someone who looked like him out on the ice. I'm glad you've gotten your chance to shine this season, although I wish it wasn't because of Drake's health issues."

Cory shakes the dad's hand. "That means a lot. Thanks for sharing."

We say goodbye to them, and as we walk away, Cory doesn't seem to be on the date with me at all. He's lost in his head.

We stop at a bar and are seated outside by the Gulf before I ask, "Are you okay?"

He takes off his hat and sunglasses, putting them on the empty chair next to him, then runs his palm over his head. "I should've said more to that little kid and his dad. I mean, 'thanks for sharing'? What a stupid response to what he told me."

"I thought it was sweet," I answer honestly.

"I started skating on ponds with my friends growing up, and there were all kinds of kids there—Black, white, Hispanic, biracial, you name it. It's all I ever knew. Then I joined a hockey team, and from there, I was probably one of two Black guys in the league. Up until then, I didn't give any thought to *who* played hockey. And once I did, I was already in love with it. I hate that Justin feels it's a white man's sport and was hesitant to try, but I get it. It's not a big part of Black culture. Beyond that, it's expensive to play hockey and not every family, especially inner-city minority families, can afford to buy new equipment when kids grow out of it so fast."

The waitress comes over and slides our drinks on the table. Cory ordered a beer, and I ordered a fruity drink with an umbrella. We order three appetizers to share and the waitress leaves.

"Did you know that Warner has a nonprofit he's opening here for kids who can't afford hockey equipment? I think I need to talk to him, see what I can do to help him out with it."

"Warner Langley?" I ask, a little surprised.

Cory laughs. "Imogen might be rich, but Warner was raised by a single mom in New York City and didn't have much growing up."

I touch his hand in an effort to ease the distress that's written all over his face. The minute our hands touch, I know it was a mistake, because a zing of electricity shoots up my arm and throughout my body. "You should then. Paying it forward. Isn't that what it's all about?"

"Yeah, I think maybe I will." He lets out a long breath.

"In the meantime, you made that kid's night. Just playing your heart out every game, you're giving kids like him something to believe in. You're showing them they can do it, that there's a spot for them."

He nods and sips his beer. "I need you around more," he says, his million-dollar smile back on display. "Now, let's talk about us."

My stomach feels queasy. For the briefest moment, I forgot that I hate Cory Freeman.

BY THE TIME we're ready to call it an evening, I'm a little buzzed from the drinks we've consumed. It wasn't my plan, but I needed the alcohol to loosen me up a bit. Being around Cory and keeping from spewing my anger at him was harder than I thought.

Cory walks me to the Uber pickup spot. He asked if he could drive me home, but I declined.

"I had a great time tonight," he says as the end of the Riverwalk comes into view.

The truth is, I did too when I forgot about this whole thing being fake. And the fact that he slept with my sister days ago. It's as if he somehow cast a magical spell on me.

"I wish I could take you home with me." He puts his hand on the small of my back, slowing our steps and leading me off to the side, out of the way of pedestrian traffic.

"Do you have no filter at all?" I ask when what I really want to ask is why my sister wasn't enough to quench his thirst on Friday night?

"I told myself I wouldn't even entertain the idea of taking you home tonight, but I'm transparent when it comes to you. I want you to know what I'm thinking. I'm not into playing games."

I barely suppress an eye roll. "Games? Who is?" I say in a defensive tone. Instantly, I clear my throat. "I mean…"

But he's quick to shush me with a finger to my lips. "I really like you, and I can't deny that I want you in my bed. I can't tell you how many times I've relived those moments we shared."

I shake my head and stare at my feet. "You need to stop."

"Why?" He lightly touches my chin with his thumb and forefinger, urging me to look up at him. "I thought you wanted to do this dating thing?"

I sigh.

"Am I missing something?" He steps back.

"No. No." The words rush out of me, surprising even myself. "Just… hearing those things makes it hard to go slow."

The corners of his lips rise in a sexy smile. "I'm ready to push down on the gas whenever you are."

"Slow down, cowboy." I raise my hand to his chest as he steps toward me. "We're still just trotting."

"Let me know when you want to ride the stallion."

I arch an eyebrow. "Don't we think highly of ourselves?"

He laughs. "Don't act like you don't remember."

An image of him naked at the edge of the bed during our vacation fling flickers to mind. His deep *V* and the grooves of his abs, not to mention all his other muscles. The wings tattooed across his chest and the light sprinkling of dark hair that travels down past his navel. And then I picture his cock. His big, rigid cock that made me come over and over again.

"Now I've made you blush." His voice is low and laced with lust.

I feel the heat on my cheeks. Cory's the last person I had sex with, and my body involuntarily sways in his direction as though I'm offering myself to him. He takes the invitation and wraps his arms around me, holding me tightly to his hard body.

"I need to go," I whisper.

"Just a second longer. The Uber will wait," he says softly in my ear. "I'm not sure what's holding you back, but I hope one day soon you'll trust me enough to talk to me about it because I'm all in on this. I feel your hesitation. But that hesitation wasn't there the other night at Warner and Imogen's wedding dinner."

I open my mouth to throw the accusation out there, but York's words ring in my ear. *"Don't fall for his games. He's a sweet talker and can make any woman swoon. Remember how many other women there probably are besides me. He's probably got a different one in every city."*

I step back from him, straightening my purse. "I gotta go. Have a great night. Thank you for the drinks and food."

I scurry away, finding my Uber before Cory can stop me. Once I'm securely in the car, Cory comes into view. He waves then blows me a kiss with a wink. Not at all fazed by me running away from him.

As I'm about to smile from the cheesiness of the situation, a group of three women swarm him. He turns and grants them the attention they seek, even posing for pictures.

I pull out my phone and send a quick text to York.

Me: *Date one is over. This is hard.*

Three dots appear.

York: *You did something right, these pictures just hit the hockey gossip blog.*

Screenshots of Cory and me pop up on my phone—us at the bar laughing, a bunch of comments suggesting I'm his next victim. One person says they hope I end up seeing this thread so I can be warned about what a player he is. Another picture pops up with a message from York right under it.

The picture shows me tucked in Cory's arms from literally minutes ago.

York: *This looks a little too cozy, sis. Watch yourself.*

She's right. You can see it written all over my face. I'm pretty sure once this is over, I might break my heart right along with Cory's.

CHAPTER 16

"I'm not his wife."
—Andi

Cory

After practice, I find a handwritten note taped to my locker from Jana Gerhardt, asking me to come see her. We're due to leave this evening for five days for a streak of away games.

"The warden calls." Tweetie reads the note over my shoulder. "You're in trouble."

Rumor is Jana is already running a lot of the office. That Mr. Gerhardt, our owner, is finding interest in other areas and one day soon, the Florida Fury will be passed down to her.

"Piss off," I say with more confidence than I feel.

I've been summoned to the executive offices and if Jana's second-in-command up there, it's probably not for the best. Usually, good news trickles down to Coach. Drake is practicing again and soon will be released to play, but I can't fathom that means they'd just get rid of me.

"Hey." Warner puts his hand on my shoulder. "Don't overthink it. I once got called up there because they wanted me to be the face of the Florida Fury. Now that you're out there making a name for yourself and I'm married with a kid on the way, it could be for the same reason."

The pressure alone if they asked me to be the face of the

franchise would crush me like a semi. I'm not built for that role.

I grab my stuff and head to the showers because Jana isn't someone you go see smelling of sweat after a practice.

"So, Imogen saw some pictures..." Warner says.

My mom saw the pictures too and called me this morning. I keep telling her to stop reading those ridiculous blog sites. All they do is upset her. But once I explained that I'd already met Ande before and she's not just a fling for me, Mom now thinks Ande could be "the one."

"You and Ande looked pretty cozy," Warner continues when I don't respond.

"Trevor's a good guy, man," Tweetie chimes in.

We all stare at him for a moment.

"You're a better guy and of course you saw her first, but I just hate to see that guy get knocked down," Tweetie adds.

Kane narrows his eyes as if he's trying to understand Tweetie but just can't. "Their relationship was a farce. All made up."

"Really?" Tweetie asks, eyes wide.

"You were there. Karaoke night? When it all went down after the kiss cam..." I stare at him, and Tweetie still has a blank expression, meaning he's lost.

"And Trevor is gay," Kane tells him.

Tweetie's jaw hangs open. "Shut up. He is not. Why was he dating Ande then?"

"Do you know what farce means?" Kane asks, forehead wrinkled.

"Yes." Tweetie puts shampoo in his hair and soap trickles down his face like a toddler.

"Then why would Trevor be upset?" Kane continues his line of questioning while I rinse soap from my body.

"He's still being denied by Ande. Imagine if some girl used you like that."

"I wouldn't give a shit if I was gay!" Kane shouts.

Tweetie lowers his head under the water, soap dripping down his face. "Oh yeah, okay. I get it now."

Kane shakes his head, but no one says anything else.

We all shower in peace until Tweetie finishes and puts a towel around his waist. "So, you're going after her, Jet?"

"I'm trying, but my goddamn past is getting in the way." I finish my shower and follow Tweetie out. "Maybe I should ask you, how the hell did you get Tedi with your reputation?"

He laughs all the way to his locker. "Because she was my fuck buddy first and things just progressed from there. I think we'd still be fuck buddies if I didn't catch feelings. That girl hides her true self through two layers of bullet-proof glass. Lucky for her, I'm persistent."

"You and your magic dick broke through the walls, huh?" Ford razzes him.

"You bet your little pecker." Tweetie tosses his hockey tape from his locker at Ford, and he dodges, so it flies right at Maksim.

"Don't get me involved in your stupid fights." Maksim throws the tape back.

"Seriously though, we've all been playboys." Tweetie sits down next to me.

A throat clearing across the room alerts me to Drake's presence.

"Okay, not you." Tweetie waves in his direction.

"Why not?" I ask Drake. "I mean, Tweetie made it seem like a rite of passage or some shit."

All the guys laugh.

"First of all, you should have never listened to Tweetie."

Drake throws on his shirt. "Second of all, you don't need to be a playboy just because you're a professional athlete. As you probably already know, it doesn't always work out for you."

He's right.

"I take that as an insult." Tweetie removes his towel without putting on his boxers, swinging his dick around. "I couldn't deny the ladies all of this."

Ford tosses him a towel and sets his gaze on me. "Listen, most of us have been where you are."

"Not me." Warner raises his hand.

"Me either." Drake raises his hand too.

Both of them wear cocky-ass smiles.

"This is easy to overcome," Ford carries on. "Just prove to her she's the one. Lena tried to play hard to get, but in the end, she couldn't deny me."

"I think it was Annabelle. She felt bad that she had you as a dad." Maksim laughs and most of the locker room joins in.

I finish getting ready while Ford throws insults at Maksim about how he had to go talk out his feelings before he got some.

Kane sits down next to me. "Just be you, Jet. I've been telling you that since you got drafted. Just be yourself and good things will follow."

I nod.

"It's clear Ande likes you, so take it slow. No need to rush." He pushes a hand through his long, wet hair.

I nod again as if I'm twelve and just got my first crush.

"But right now, go see Jana because this is what is most important in your life."

Kane's right. Hockey comes first. I'm too early in my career to jeopardize it for anything. Drake, Maksim, Ford,

Warner, they've all been in the league for years. Proven their worth. This is my time to shine, and I'm focused on Ande.

I shake my head. "You're right. Thanks."

I grab my stuff and head out of the locker room, still hearing the others arguing about who was the bigger playboy in their day.

I KNOCK on Jana's closed office door, hearing laughter inside.

"Come in," she says, and I open the door to find Ande on the couch across from where Jana sits in a chair. Jana isn't wearing her usual heels and she's sitting cross-legged, sipping a glass of what looks like sparkling water. "Cory, please." She sweeps her hand, directing me to sit next to Ande.

I smile at Ande, but she flicks her gaze back to Jana.

"We were just talking about Trevor and the kiss cam." Jana laughs again.

"Oh," I say, sitting down next to Ande. She's wearing jeans and a sweater that shows off her awesome figure. "You don't work today?"

She glances at her watch. "Trevor gave me an extra-long lunch."

Her demeanor is not what I thought it would be after last night. I meant what I told her. She's holding back on me, and I hope that she tells me what it is that's keeping her walls up after she decided to give us a shot.

"Okay, you two." Jana clicks a button on a remote and a screen comes down from the ceiling in the middle of the room.

She clicks another button and the blog post my mom saw last night comes up. The puck bunnies questioning who

Ande is. Them saying they've never seen me look at another woman like I look at Ande. I hate these fucking things, but I'll give them props on figuring that out.

But Jana doesn't give us much time to look it over before she changes the screen. "Then there's this."

We stare at some other hockey gossip blog about married hockey players and their kids. Ford, Lena, and Annabelle pictured at a park.

"I'll be honest with you two. I thought women wanted their crushes single, so they knew if they ran into them one day, they'd have a chance to fall in love like some Hallmark movie. But Warner Langley proved me wrong. He got more hype after outing his relationship with Imogen than he did before it was common knowledge. A fan started this blog to report who's seeing who and the crazy thing is that it's positive. The more the guy is in love, or at least shows his love for a woman, the more they get on here. They actually rank the guys on who is the better husband."

I glance at Ande, wondering what this has to do with us, but she's looking at the screen, hands clenched on her lap.

Jana clicks on a picture of Imogen at a game with a shirt that says, "Growing a little number thirty-four" on her belly. "This alone put Warner up to number one for a week above all the other players in the league. In truth, Ford and Warner are competing regularly for the top two spots. Now, Cory, I don't think I have to remind you that you've made some sketchy decisions between the end of last year and now."

Jana changes the screen again, and neither Ande nor I say anything. The picture shows Ande and me last night. Her in my arms and the caption reading, "Could Cory Freeman win our hearts after all?"

"They like this, so we like it too." She turns off the screen and it rolls back up into the ceiling as she looks pointedly at us. "My question is, what's going on between you two?"

"Um," Ande says and glances in my direction.

I slide closer and take her hand. "We're dating."

"It's casual," Ande clarifies.

"Monogamous?" Jana leans back and crosses her arms.

"For me, yes," Ande says.

My head whips in her direction, forehead creased. I squeeze her limp hand. "For me too."

Jana claps. "I'm so happy to hear that. I was so hopeful."

"Why?" Ande asks, clearly confused.

"Because Cory needs to maintain the trajectory of his career and we need him to clean up his reputation since he's spending time on the starting lineup. Which makes this easier since you're already dating."

"It's casual though," Ande says—again.

I glance at her, wondering where all this is coming from.

"All we need is neither of you dating anyone else."

"Jana, what are you asking us to do?" Ande takes the lead on this discussion for the two of us.

"Nothing. Just be yourselves, but make sure you get out there in public. Let them take pictures. I'm thinking you should accompany Cory on an away game because that shows commitment. Most of the other wives travel—"

Ande laughs. "I'm not his wife."

"Tedi, who is also not a wife, travels with Tweetie a lot. We'll play it by ear. All I needed to know is that you two are monogamous. I don't want this blowing up in our faces." She steadies her gaze on me. "You can do this, right, Cory?"

Ande's hand turns clammy in mine.

I narrow my eyes at Jana, insulted that she thinks she needs to keep clarifying whether I can maintain monogamy.

"I'm one hundred percent in this, but I'm unsure what my personal life has to do with my hockey career."

Jana laughs and shakes her head. "Rookies are so cute." Then she sobers up. "My job is to fill the seats in that arena. Get merchandise out the door. Seats don't sell, and guess what? We can't pay players. Then you're playing on a crappy team who never wins. You'll try for a trade, you're probably thinking? Let me ask you, do you think a team is more interested in a playboy who is out partying all night and getting bad press or the family man who goes home and takes care of himself? Teams want solutions, not problems."

She makes a good argument. I nod reluctantly. "Kane said I need to think about my career right now."

I swear a sound comes out of Ande, but she masks it.

"Then listen to me and I'll make sure you have an excellent career." Jana grins at me.

Ande stands. "Is that all?"

Jana's eyes widen. "Are you okay?"

Ande nods a little too much. "Yeah, but I have to get back to work."

"Okay, maybe find some dates that work for you to attend an away game," Jana says. "The team will cover the cost."

"Sure." Ande turns to me. "I'll see you later."

"Hold up, I'll walk you out." I stand.

"I'm fine. No worries." Ande rushes out the door.

"If I was you, I'd make sure she's okay with this arrangement. Something's up with her." Jana points toward the door.

She's right, so I bolt out the door to find Ande, but she's gone by the time I reach the elevator.

CHAPTER 17

Andie

As soon as I detour into the stairwell, I take a moment to draw a breath. I've never hyperventilated before, but that meeting with Jana made me feel as though the walls were closing in on all sides.

Knowing I don't have much time, I jog down the rest of the steps until I open the door to the outside. A burst of Florida sunshine hits my eyes and I squint. I'm not at the parking lot where I parked my car. I walk around the building, crossing my fingers Cory doesn't pop out from around a corner. I could tell he wanted to talk to me, but I need to gather my thoughts.

Once I'm in my car and driving out of the Fury parking lot, I dial up York on my Bluetooth.

"What's up, Mrs. Freeman?" Her tone is sarcastic and laced with annoyance.

"I was just at the Florida Fury office." I check my blind spot and switch lanes.

"And?"

"And Jana Gerhardt, the owner's daughter, likes that our picture was taken and made it onto the gossip sites. I guess there's some new trend in the popularity of hockey players in relationships." Even I hear the panic in my voice.

"Relax, Ande. You sound like you just snorted five lines of cocaine."

I grip the steering wheel tighter and continue to talk. I should've talked to Trevor about this plan York concocted. He would have talked me out of it. He thinks I'm seeing Cory because I want to. York said the more people we told, the more likely the truth would come out, so I've kept the plan to myself.

"This is good for us," York says.

"How do you figure?"

"Because this way we can stick it to him publicly. How satisfying will that be? Maybe we should do some big reveal with the two of us together and make him squirm." The vindictive tone in her voice is something I've heard many times before.

"I don't know, York..." I turn onto the street toward my office.

"Don't wimp out on me now. What did Jana say exactly?"

"She wants us to be seen in public. She wants me to go to an away game. Said it would show our commitment. The other wives go."

"So you're in wife territory now?" I don't miss the snip in her voice.

"Girlfriends, I mean. And will you stop sounding so sour? I don't think I'm the kind of person who can handle this sort of thing."

She blows out a breath. "Stop selling yourself short. Remember how you threw up after you found out Cory slept with me? Imagine how many other women he did that to and made feel that way and then he's trying to act like some Prince Charming? Give me a break."

I nod although she can't see me. Just the image of him with York sends bile up my throat.

"This is perfect. I'm telling you, he'll learn his lesson when it goes public and people witness his heartbroken ass." She laughs almost manically, and I have to remind myself she was played too.

"So I'm doing this?" I ask, pulling into the parking lot of my work and wishing I could talk to Trevor about this. He's been my best friend since I moved here. I love that my sister and I are talking more than we ever have, but something in my gut feels off.

"Yes, you're doing this!" She's silent for a moment. "I mean, I don't want to push you into it. If you'd rather let every guy walk all over you and get away with it, that's your business. I just didn't think you were a doormat. Michael took you for a ride. You thought you were going to marry him, and bang, he cheats and drops you. Now Cory is spouting lies and trying to make you think you're his one and only."

She's right. "Okay, should I call him?"

"Didn't you talk to him when you were with Jana?"

"I freaked out and made the excuse that I had to get to work. He's going to be gone for five days playing away games."

"Ha! I bet he's hooking up when he's away."

My stomach sours, but I don't say anything, taking the keys out of the ignition and switching her from my Bluetooth to just speaker.

"Ande, I know this isn't normally something you'd do. You're a lot better person than I am, but sometimes you have to stand up for yourself and teach people a lesson. I think Cory Freeman needs to learn he can't use women when he feels like it and cast them aside when he's done with them."

"I just wish it could be you. You're so much better equipped for something like this."

She chuckles. "I would've if he didn't..." She stops talking and I hear someone behind her. "Listen, I gotta go, but I'll call you tonight. I was thinking after this is over, maybe we plan a vacation. Just the two of us, a beach, and fruity umbrella drinks. If we're lucky, we'll pick up two hot brothers or something."

I've always wondered what it would be like to be close to York and I can't help the warm feeling in my chest, picturing the two of us away together and having fun. "That would be nice."

"Just hang in there. From the look of those pictures, it won't take you long. Looks like you almost have him there."

"Where?" I ask.

"Where Cory Freeman is madly in love with you. Gotta go, talk to you later. Love you."

The line dies and I sit in my car for a moment. Shaking my head, I open the door and head back into the office. Hopefully work will distract me for a few hours.

I'm WATCHING another reality TV show where people are searching for love. This time they have to date but can't see each other, only get to know each other by talking. I wonder if I could ever go on a show like that. Looks aren't that important to me in a partner, though Cory is sexy as hell. But he's not a good man. What I wouldn't do for a wholesome, honest man in my life.

My phone buzzes next to me, so I put down my bowl of popcorn to see a text from Cory.

Cory: *I wanted to check in on you earlier but had to catch a flight. We're in New York. Are you OK?*

Me: *I'm fine.*

Cory: *Can I call you or are you out?*

Me: *It's Monday night. I'm not out singing karaoke and doing shots.*

MY PHONE RINGS a few seconds after I send the text.

"Hello," I answer.

"Hey, beautiful." His voice is deep and sultry and smooth.

"Did you play tonight?"

"No, tomorrow, but we had to get here early for practice tomorrow and then a game. I wanted to talk to you about the Jana thing and see where your head was at."

I pause my show and place my popcorn bowl on the coffee table. I guess I can be honest with him about this much. "I know I freaked. It's just the thought of everyone knowing my business, or worse, being judged. Plus, you know my fears..." I want to give him an opportunity to come clean.

"About me messing with other girls?"

"Yeah. I know what you said, but..." I pick at a piece of fluff on my sock.

"Right now, I'm alone in my hotel room while most of my teammates are out. Not because I'm trying to prove a point or because of what Jana said about my reputation but because for the entire day, I've been waiting for the moment I could message you. I'd rather talk to you than go clubbing any day of the week."

I wish I could believe his words. "You don't have to lie to me."

"Jeez, you make it hard to be truthful."

I swallow a gulp from my glass of wine. "I told you this is why we shouldn't even try. I'm not ready to date someone with such a presence in front of the world."

"World?" He chuckles. "That's not even close to reality."

"You know what I mean. Usually my dating life only involves one other person. This feels like a setup for a public heart lashing."

"Always the skeptic. We might actually make it."

Guilt floods my bloodstream and makes my heart rate pick up. If all goes to plan, he'll be the one getting the public heart lashing. Unless I'm dumb enough to fall for him again.

Cory groans.

"What's that for?" I figure changing the topic is a safer bet.

"Just getting up off the bed. I ran into the boards today and gave myself a wicked bruise on my side."

"Did you ice it?"

"Yeah, but honestly, it was my own fucking fault. My mind was other places."

"Oh."

He chuckles. "You don't want to know where it was?"

"I didn't want to pry."

"It's with you, Ande. My mind is always on you lately."

My heart flutters like butterfly wings before I remind myself not to believe anything he says. We do not allow our heart to flutter where Cory is concerned.

"Oh, that's nice," I say like an idiot because I have no idea how to respond. "How bad is your side?"

"I've had worse. Maybe when I get back, you can nurse me back to health." He groans again. "Just sitting back down on my bed. I got room service and forgot to eat my cheesecake."

"Must be nice eating cheesecake you know you'll burn off tomorrow."

"The joys of playing hockey, but I still shouldn't eat this crap. I should be eating vegetables and lean protein."

I've seen the guys eat at Carmelo's and not one of them watches what they eat. "I say eat it now while you're young."

He laughs. "You say that like you're old."

We're roughly the same age. "Sometimes I feel like I'm fifty. Especially after my dad died."

He groans and moans a few more times. "I'm just getting comfortable. You can talk a little longer, right?"

I glance at the clock. It's only nine o'clock. "I should go to bed. I have this file I need to complete tomorrow—"

"Just a few minutes. Please?"

The man is hurt. I guess I can put up this charade a little longer tonight.

"You mentioned your sister visiting the other day and I was wondering if you have any other siblings besides your sister?"

Just the word sister coming out of his mouth makes me see red. All I envision is him and York in bed together.

"No, just the sister." I do my best to keep my voice light.

"Are you two close?"

"Um... not really. We're pretty different." That's been the truth in the past, but I'm hoping this whole plan brings us closer. It would be nice if something good could come out of it.

"That sucks. I always wanted siblings, but by the time my parents had me, they were older, and my mom always said they were lucky to have me with her old eggs."

"Siblings aren't all they're cracked up to be. Sure, I had a playmate, but she was more like my enemy most of the time. I yearned for an older brother. One who watched over me, you know?"

In reality, any sibling who would've helped me with our dad would have been better than my sister, who ignored the situation. I just always figured if it was a brother, he would've been able to handle it better than me. At the very least he would've looked out for me while I was looking out for my dad.

"Well, since I learned how to play chess at the age of four, I'd say you had it better."

"Didn't you have friends?"

"I did, but you know how many nights it was just my parents and me? On the positive side, I can play all the old-people games like chess, bridge, and Parcheesi."

I can't help the laugh that bubbles out of me. "Parcheesi sounds like it belongs in a retirement center."

"You'd be right. Sometimes I feel as old as my parents. And you know what comes from having older parents?"

"What?" I lie down on my couch and pull my blanket over me.

"A lot of lectures. When you're their only child and they have decades of life experience, they have nothing but time for you. Add on the hockey element and I feel like I lived at our kitchen table."

"What would they lecture you about?"

He huffs. "Everything from being a good teammate, to what you can learn from losing, to how schoolwork comes first, treat girls with respect, don't kiss and tell. The list is endless."

A sad smile forms on my lips. I never had any of that. By the time I got old enough for boys, my dad was already addicted and didn't care much for anything but how he was going to score pills. I navigated that world all by myself.

"I'd like to hear about your childhood sometime. I mean, if you're willing to share."

I inhale deeply, unsure I want to answer that question. "Maybe some other time. I'm sorry, Cory, I'm exhausted. Talk to you later?"

"Already, huh?" He pauses. "Okay. I'm glad I got to hear your voice before I went to bed."

"Good night," I say, ignoring the bulk of what he said.

"Good night, beautiful."

I'm quick to hang up, and with my phone on my chest, I stare at my ceiling. Between York and me, we definitely picked the wrong person to run Operation Break Cory Freeman's Heart. I can already feel myself softening toward him.

CHAPTER 18

*"Will you come into tonight with
an open heart and mind?"*
-Cory

Cory

After our game the next night, a few of the guys want to go to an expensive steak house to celebrate our win.

We head to someplace Ford knows and are seated in a curtained-off room for privacy. As we walked through the rows of people dressed in suits and elegant dresses, we got a few glances but not much more. I heard someone say Ford's name, but who knows if they recognize him for being a hockey star or for being a member of the Jacobs family.

Once we're seated, I realize how odd it feels for us to be out without any of the wives or girlfriends. Saige comes a lot since she's everyone's social media manager, and usually if Saige comes, Tedi comes too.

I send a text to Ande since my good morning text didn't get answered. She's been distant since the whole Jana thing. I didn't think Ande would like to be public with me, so I'd planned on keeping our relationship behind closed doors as much as possible, but I guess at some point if we work out, she'll have to get used to the attention, the pictures, and unfortunately, the criticism.

Me: *Hey, how was your day?*

"Did everyone see who's number one on the married list?" Ford winks, lifting his glass like a king.

"Don't worry, tomorrow it'll be me. Imogen is flying into town, and she'll be in the stands. And we may or may not have another T-shirt ready to go."

Ford shakes his head. "You're selling out your own kid."

"It's for the fans. Plus, she's started to show a little."

Ford laughs. "I saw her yesterday, man. She looks like she ate too much at the buffet."

While they argue, I check my phone when I feel it vibrate in my pocket.

Ande: *It was okay. Sorry about not getting back to you this morning, I woke up late and it was a hectic day.*

Me: *You don't have to apologize. I'm at dinner with the guys and I was wondering if you'd be up later for me to call.*

The three dots appear and disappear.

"This is guys' time, Jet, get off the damn phone," Tweetie says.

I ignore him because the guys are on their phones plenty of times during dinners like these.

"Give him a break, he's in the new love phase," Aiden says. "I remember I couldn't get enough of Saige. Hell, I still can't, but I was lucky to have her travel with us."

"And how was that?" I ask.

Aiden tilts his head. "You thinking about asking Ande to travel with the team?"

I shrug.

"Well, Saige did it because she was my social media content person. But I fucking loved it. She still comes a lot because I like to explore the cities I'm in. Who would've thought a kid from Wisconsin could end up traveling all over the place?" He picks up his drink and sips it, shaking his head. "Now I just have to get my position back." He winks at me.

We both know it's only a matter of time. He'll get cleared within the next week or so and I'll be off the first line.

I glance at my phone.

Ande: *Um... depends how late.*

Me: *How about if you go to bed before you hear from me, you just text me.*

Ande: *Sure.*

Me: *Although I really want to hear your voice. You want to send me a seductive voicemail I can listen to over and over again?*

I include a laughing GIF.

Ande: *Maybe another time. Talk to you later... maybe.*

Me: *I hope so.*

That ends our conversation. I have no idea where we stand, and it sucks I'm on the road for the next four nights.

For the rest of the evening, the guys banter and compete over everything from who can eat the rarest steak to who's gonna be the next to get their girl pregnant.

Ford points at me. "It better not be you, Jet."

I point at myself, forehead wrinkled, wondering why he's calling me out.

"You're not ready. Give yourself time."

"You got Lena and she thinks of Annabelle as her own," I say.

"She *is* her mom. She's the only mom Annabelle will probably ever know. That's why I'm saying you gotta give your relationship some time."

Warner leans back and laughs. "Who would've ever thought Ford Jacobs would be giving advice on relationships? Unbelievable."

Ford throws a roll at Warner, which he catches and takes a bite out of.

"Just a friendly warning." Ford winks.

After we're done eating, we stand to leave, and when we get outside, there's a group of women who swarm us. They call us by our names or nicknames, asking for pictures. Women are asking about Annabelle, and someone even gives Ford a shirt that says, "My daddy is the hottest hockey player in the league"—which he shows to Warner with a smug smile.

I sign a few sheets of paper before our cars arrive and we pile in to escape the mayhem. Once we're in the car, no one says anything about what just went down, as though it's an everyday occurrence. Maybe it's because I just got into the starting line and people are recognizing me more, but I've never experienced anything like that. I'm starting to realize how it can fuck up a relationship real quick.

<hr>

SATURDAY MORNING, I head over to the coffee shop to grab a coffee and breakfast sandwich because I'm still recovering from our five-day away game stint. It's amazing how little rest I get in a hotel bed.

I sit at a table by the window as a little boy and his mom

walk in. It's clear he knows who I am right away—his mouth hangs open and he's tugging on his mom's arm—but she's busy trying to order for them.

I smile to myself because there have been times when my teammates were recognized and kids approached them while I stood on the sidelines.

The mom picks up her coffee and he takes his chocolate milk from her, then she hands him a bag with a pastry, and they sit a few tables down from me. He keeps checking on me while I finish eating my sandwich and sip my coffee. I look out the window and do a double take when I see Ande walking down the other side of the street. I get up from my seat, and of course, the kid takes that moment to talk to me.

"Jet Freeman?" he asks in a small, insecure voice.

I turn to him and his smile grows, but I'm torn because if I stay back to chat with him, I'll never catch Ande. The kid stands and his mom touches his arm to stop him. He explains who I am, and she nods, smiling at me. Then she digs in her purse. What would this world do without moms? Always prepared for anything.

"Hey, buddy, what's your name?"

He introduces himself and the mom comes over for me to sign my autograph for him. I ask him if he plays ice hockey. Down here in Florida, more kids street skate than ice skate, but he surprises me with a yes.

"We're originally from Minnesota. My husband was transferred down here," the mom explains.

"Well, keep on skating and working hard," I tell him and give him a fist bump.

"Thank you so much," the mom says. "He's a huge fan of Florida Fury."

"Who's your favorite?" I ask with a smile.

The kid glances down and I automatically know it's not me. "Aiden Drake."

I laugh at the mom's look of embarrassment. "He's a great guy and you'll see him back on the ice soon."

I say my goodbyes and turn to leave, but find Ande right inside the doorway, staring at me. She's wearing jeans and a T-shirt with an open sweatshirt over top. Her hair is tossed into a messy ponytail and she's not wearing any makeup.

I swear I fall for her all over again. This is what she'd look like if we woke up on a regular Saturday together. I picture myself suggesting we find a small coffee shop and read the paper while we eat pastries.

"Hey, beautiful."

She blushes as she often does when I use that word. "Are you stalking me? You're on my side of town."

"Maybe you're on mine," I say, approaching her.

She steps into line, and I stay at her side. "Where do you live?"

"Just up the street."

"Stop messing with me," she says and gets one person closer to placing her order.

"I'm not. I swear." I hold up both hands. "You mean to tell me we live by one another and have never run into each other?"

She shakes her head. "I guess not. I figured you lived with all the other hockey players in that fancy neighbor-hood on the beach."

"Nah, I'm more of a lie low kinda guy. Plus I'm a rookie, remember?"

In truth, I'm a rookie who got one hell of a signing bonus, but I'm not going to be one of those idiots who blows it all and retires with nothing.

The barista asks for the next in line and Ande orders a

latte with soy milk, and I order another coffee black. Before she can pay, I beat her to the punch.

"Cory," she sighs.

I shake my head and accept my change, putting some of the bills in the tip jar. We walk down the counter and wait for our drinks.

"I'm glad I ran into you," I say. "Are you still available tonight?"

"Tonight?" It's almost as if she's trying to find an excuse, so she surprises me when she says, "Yes, I am."

"Great. Can I take you sailing? I mean, not me, someone who actually knows what he's doing would man the ship. We'd have dinner and see the sunset."

She stares at me for a beat then nods. "Sure."

"Great." I smile at her.

Our drinks are ready, so I pick them both up and hand over hers. We head outside and I walk alongside her as we walk through the small downtown area of our town. There are cute shops and restaurants around a square that gives the area a small-town vibe.

"Does that happen often?" she asks, eyeing my coffee cup.

Confused, I look down and see there's a phone number written on the side of my cup, the name Erin scrawled below it. "Occupational hazard?"

She laughs and shakes her head. "How do you fend off all these women, Cory Freeman?"

I stop her in front of a clothing store. "Easy. I only have eyes for one."

She holds my gaze for a long time and bites her lower lip. It makes me want to lean in and kiss her, but something tells me she wouldn't welcome it right now.

"Cory," she says in that tone that tells me she's fighting this connection we clearly have.

"What?"

"How can you give up all those women for me?"

God, I hate what that asshole ex has done to her. Making her doubt every guy who's come after him. "I think it's time for me to show you. Will you come into tonight with an open heart and mind?"

I watch her chest rise and fall, waiting for her answer because she has a wall I haven't been able to bust through. She could easily say no.

"Yes," she says.

I step closer, tucking the one strand of hair that's come loose from her ponytail behind her ear. "I'll pick you up at five. Text me your address?"

"Okay," she says.

I desperately want to kiss her, but I refrain, hoping tonight will be the night.

I stare into her eyes for a beat longer to let her know I'm serious. I'm going to prove her worth to her. There's no one on this planet I'd rather be with than her, and I know she feels the same way about me. I just have to disprove everything that jackass made her believe.

"See you tonight," I say and walk away.

"Bye."

As hard as it is to leave her right now, it has to be done. Maybe she's gotta miss me a little bit to want me.

CHAPTER 19

Andie

Cory doesn't show up at five; he shows up at four forty-five. A full fifteen minutes early. So I have to open the door with my hair half curled. Even if the wind on the sailboat takes out all the curls, I might as well start my date looking good. I'm supposed to be getting him to fall for me after all, even if I am doing a shit job so far.

He hands me flowers, and I blush from the fact that it's such a Date 101 move, yet it still makes my heart pitter-patter.

"Thank you. I'll put them in water once I'm done getting ready. You're early."

"Feel lucky I didn't show up hours ago." He laughs and walks into my kitchen. "Where's the vase? I'll put them in water." He starts opening cabinets.

"Have you ever heard of privacy?"

He laughs. "Sorry. I sorta feel like we're past that already. Maybe because we hooked up on vacation. Just show me." He stands in the middle of my kitchen, waiting for me to tell him.

"The cabinet to the left of the stove. I'm going to finish getting ready." I head down the hall to finish curling my hair.

"Not sure I like all the vases you have in here." I hear

him chuckle. "Tell me you collect them and it's not all from flower deliveries from other men."

"I just like vases. Most of the time I'm buying my own flowers." I say it loud enough for him to hear me down the hall while I curl my hair, smiling into the mirror when I shouldn't be.

York called me earlier, and I didn't even tell her I was going out with Cory because I didn't want to hear from her how I should act.

"Not anymore. I can arrange flowers to be delivered weekly for you," he shouts back. Then I hear the water running.

I finish getting ready and come back out to the kitchen to find that he's trimmed each stem and arranged the flowers in a vase in a way that looks professional.

"Am I missing something?"

"Like?" He tilts his head.

"Like, did you consider being a florist in case hockey didn't work out for you?"

He laughs and I hate that I love that sound more every day. "My mom likes flowers too. She taught me how to keep them alive longer." He leans toward me and whispers, "Lemon-lime soda, in case you're wondering."

"Thank you for the tip."

"You're welcome." He walks around the counter and his eyes eat me up. "You're gorgeous."

I glance down at my sundress with a sweater over top in case it gets cold, even though the weather has been great lately. "Thank you and you..." He's wearing a pair of khaki pants and a button-down with the sleeves rolled up so some of his ink is showing. "You look very handsome."

"Then I think the most stunning couple in Florida should head out so we can be admired." He offers me his arm, and I slide my arm through his, letting him lead the way.

He drives us to the marina. When we step out, only one sailboat has its lights lit up. It's not at all small and I find myself excited to get on board. It seems so romantic.

Cory takes my hand and I wish it didn't spark an electric current inside me. Michael never romanced me. I always chalked it up to the fact that we met as poor college kids, but I realize now he could've done things on a smaller scale. Cory has the money to romance me with things most men can't replicate, and I have to remind myself not to let it work. It's supposed to be the other way around.

As we approach the sailboat, I see a woman standing there with two champagne glasses. She asks us to take off our shoes since neither of us are wearing proper deck shoes and they don't want the boat damaged.

I slip out of my heels and walk onto the wooden deck, with Cory's help. I accept a champagne glass, walk up the ramp, and come face-to-face with who I assume is the captain. At least there are a lot of stripes on his white uniform. Other members of the crew come and introduce themselves, but the woman who handed us the champagne, Becky, is our server for the evening.

She escorts us to the top area of the boat—which I'm sure has a name I don't know. We're seated at a small table for two with lights that look like candles spread all over.

After Becky leaves, I whisper, "Cory, this is a lot."

"No such thing when it comes to you. Plus, this gives us some privacy, which I know you want."

"But—"

He shakes his head. "You've been closed off with me since the Jana thing. I know being involved with me isn't easy. Especially with Jana wanting us to be public about our relationship. I figure we can change it up for tonight and she'll be none the wiser." He winks.

I don't say anything. Mostly because Jana's wishes aren't the only reason I was upset this week. I'm trying to close off any feelings I'm developing for him and he's not making it easy.

"How did you know?" I ask.

But Becky interrupts us with a shrimp appetizer and rolls. Cory dishes me out some of the appetizer and I pass him the rolls.

"You think I don't know you, but I do. The connection I felt with you on that island is still there for me. And I know you well enough to know you don't like the attention I garner, especially from women."

I move my shrimp around my plate because I want to blurt out, "You slept with my sister and god knows how many other women when you were trying to convince me I meant something more to you." Instead, I say, "Can I ask you a question?"

"Anything. I'm not bullshitting you. Ask me anything."

He seems so eager to let me in. He's like the opposite of me.

"The other women... your reputation after our fling."

He winces at the word fling, but that's what it was.

"Why?"

He wipes his mouth and leans back in his seat. "I'm not sure I have a perfect answer."

"An honest one will do." I hold his stare.

"You weren't answering my calls, so I figured I was exactly that, a fling, to you. I'm embarrassed to say how much that bruised my ego. A few of the guys told me to live it up while I could. I think I got caught up in the mentality and stereotypes of professional athletes and it seemed like a good way to try to get you out of my head. And honestly, the women make it easy." He shrugs.

An expression must cross my face that signals that everything he's saying is my worst nightmare because he's quick to interject before I can.

"I was young and stupid."

"It wasn't that long ago," I deadpan.

"Yeah, it wasn't, but it was before you came back into my life. And I know what a cop-out that sounds like, believe me. But I didn't have you then. Or any other woman in my life, so temptation and persistence won. That wouldn't happen now."

I fork a shrimp and hold it up. "What makes you so sure?"

"Look at me," he says, and I stare at him. The purple-and-pink sky behind him makes him seem like a dream. As though this is all a dream. "I wish you could crawl inside me and feel what I feel for you because then you'd have no doubt. I know trust is a big thing for you and I'm trying to earn it, but I need you to loosen the grip just a little. Give me the benefit of the doubt."

"How many?" I ask because if he knew I know what I do, he'd know why I can't give him the benefit of the doubt.

"Women?"

"Yeah."

He looks chagrined, and I roll my eyes. "I'm gonna be honest. I've had regulars in a few cities, but for the most part—"

I raise my hand. "Never mind, I don't want to know." God, what a stupid masochistic question to ask.

He takes my hand. "They meant nothing. I know that's a superficial, playboy thing to say, and believe me, my mom would kick my ass to the moon if she heard me say that, but it's the truth. And none of them wanted me for me. They liked the idea of sleeping with an athlete, bragging to their friends that they got me. I'm like a prize from one of those crane games."

I laugh. "You're honestly comparing those two things?"

"Have you ever played them? They're fucking impossible."

"I've seen five-year-olds win."

He chuckles and shakes his head. "Well, I can't win at them. And look how much people brag when they do win. It's the same with sleeping with professional athletes."

"So you're like a stuffed rabbit?" I raise an eyebrow.

"Kind of. Yes."

"Interesting concept."

Luckily, Becky comes back out and puts a bowl of lobster bisque on our serving plates.

"I swear to you—"

I shake my head. "I believe you. I can't imagine having gorgeous men at my feet, begging me to sleep with them. Maybe I'd have done the same."

"I'm sure you have a lot of admirers. You certainly have one desperate man begging at your feet."

My cheeks feel like they're on fire. "Okay, next subject."

Throughout dinner, we talk more about him playing hockey. How being an only child probably helped him achieve his goal. His parents didn't have to allocate money to a sibling's extracurriculars and he had their undivided attention.

By the time dessert comes, I laugh when I see Becky bringing out cheesecake. "Did you special order this?"

He shrugs with a grin. "I love cheesecake."

"So the way to your heart is—"

"Cheesecake. Top ten for sure." He forks his piece and holds it in front of my mouth. "Do you like it?"

"Yes." I open my mouth and he slides the fork in. He watches my lips with rapt attention.

"Let me feed you the rest of my slice?"

I laugh. "We're not one of those *cheesy* couples."

"Then one more piece," he begs, and I nod.

I've never liked being fed like a child, but the way he looks at me when the fork slides back out of my mouth and my tongue dips out between my lips... maybe I've been missing out.

Becky comes over and tells us that anytime we're ready, we can retreat to the cushioned booths, that there are some blankets there. Cory finishes his cheesecake and I eat half of mine, offering the rest to Cory, who accepts happily.

After we're finished, Cory takes our wine and my hand, leading me to the cushions. We get comfy and he wraps a blanket over my lap. "Are you cold?"

"Not too bad."

He tsks. "Damn, I was hoping you were so I could offer some body heat."

I shouldn't. It's crossing a line, but I am trying to make him think I'm falling for him. So I open the blanket and his eyes widen before he quickly gets underneath it with me. His arm wraps around my shoulder, and he urges me to lean back on his chest. We stare at the sky and watch the sun descend.

Music plays—soft country he must've requested for me. "Chasing After You" by Ryan Hurd and Maren Morris comes on and I swear his arms tighten around me. I listen to the lyrics and hope he didn't pick this song because it's all too much like us. Is that what we're destined for? Him to chase and me continuing to run? Taking York out of the mix, am I even capable of loving a man in the public eye? It would mean having to hand over so much trust, and I'm not sure I have it in me.

At some point, we'll part and I'm sure he'll find some woman who loves the limelight and is secure in herself. I'm just not her.

CHAPTER 20

"C'mere. Let me comfort you a little."

Cory

It's been a few weeks since Ande agreed to start seeing me. For the most part, we don't see a lot of each other during the week, but she's agreed to a date every weekend so far, depending on my schedule. I try to think of unique places to take her, but the list is growing shorter. She doesn't seem too keen on hanging out at one of our houses —probably because we haven't been physical yet. Which I'm not upset about. I want her to feel comfortable. But if and when she says the word, I'm ready.

Today we're going for a group deep-sea fishing excursion that Jana set up. She wants to get shots of some of the Florida Fury couples. But she also invited Kane. Jana will be in attendance too—supposedly to make sure we all behave and that she gets the pictures she wants. Kane is tight lipped whenever Jana's name comes up, but I swear something is going on between them.

We're the last ones to pull up to the marina, and Jana gives me a look like I brought a hooker and not Ande. It's not my fault. Ande was confused on what to wear and I wasn't much help since I've never been fishing, let alone deep-sea fishing.

"Jet!" Tweetie shouts. "For having that nickname, you're not too speedy."

Ande raises her hand. "Completely my fault. I wish I would've asked what to wear."

She's in jeans, winter boots she probably wore in Salt Lake City, and four layers of shirts from sweatshirt to tank top. In her bag, she has hair ties, sunglasses, a hat, and reading material.

"Oh, we're not fishing," Imogen says and corrals Ande closer to the women. "The men catch our food."

"Holy shit, did my feminist sister just say that?" Ford hollers with laughter.

"I think I need to clean out my ears." Warner goes along with it, and Imogen gives him the look and runs her hand across her belly like a silent warning. But Warner keeps it up. "I thought I was going to lounge back and you'd be catching our dinner."

Imogen shakes her head and drags Ande to the women.

"I'd like you all to partake. I think there could be some funny pictures," Jana, always thinking of business, says.

Everyone heads down the pier, but Jana stays back by me, and I prepare for a lashing.

"I wanted to tell you, it's working great. I checked the blogs after your last date. Good job on the music festival, by the way. A lot of pictures were taken, and the puck bunnies are eating it up. They're loving you two as a couple. It's really turning that reputation you gave yourself around."

I shove my hands in my pockets and nod. "That's good."

Jana isn't the reason I'm taking Ande places. I'm picking spots I think she'd enjoy and we can have fun together. I hate the stares, the pictures, and the interruptions as much as Ande does, I think. Sometimes I feel as if she's just waiting for some girl to approach us and tell me she's pregnant with my baby.

When we're alone, that wall of hers gets lowered about

halfway. We talk about more intimate things, including our childhoods. She's even told me a little more about her ex. I'd really like a few minutes alone in a room with that jackass.

"Now we up the game. In two weeks, you're on an away game stint. Someone with your money who has a woman he loves wouldn't leave her behind that long. So, Ande needs to come to at least one away game. I'd prefer her to follow you along to another city though, so I've arranged it so that Saige and Tedi will be there as well. They can all do some shopping or something, show how she's bonding with the other wives and girlfriends."

I stop us before we reach the boat. "I'll mention it to her, but she has her own life, you know. I hate how orchestrated this whole thing is. Makes it seem like we're participating in something that's not real. Something dishonest."

Jana laughs. "Press and PR are part of being a professional hockey player." She pats my shoulder.

"And when will it stop?"

She shrugs. "Marry the girl."

I give her a look that says if Ande and I were getting married, it would not be up for public consumption. "You're already publicizing the rest of the couples. Why do you need me?"

She shrugs. "We're just capitalizing on it because of that blog, but I'll be honest, Cory, this is new territory for me. I always thought the puck bunnies liked the single guys. If someone had bet me how into real relationships this generation is, I'd probably be dirt poor." She puts her hand on my forearm and squeezes. "Hang in there. You're definitely falling for each other. Pictures don't lie."

She gets on the boat, and I catch Ande's eye and I can tell she wants to know what we were talking about. I shake my head that it's no big deal and she continues her conversation with the girls.

THE SUN IS OUT and intense. Sweat pours down my forehead, through my shirt, and all I want to do is jump in the ocean. We have all our fishing poles in holders, waiting to see a tug on a line so we can try to be the first to snag a fish. Warner and Ford are, of course, taking it to a whole different level of competition.

"I was this close to bringing the filet mignon from last night's dinner as bait," Ford says.

"Filet mignon isn't going to bring the fish in." Warner shakes his head, propping his feet up on the ledge of the boat, reclined as though he doesn't care. We've all abandoned our poles a time or two, but Warner watches his intensely, waiting for some action.

"You know a watched pot doesn't boil," Tweetie says, and we all stare at him. "What? That adage works."

"I'm going to check on my girl," Maksim leaves.

"Me too." Aiden joins him.

"Hey, I wanted to warn you that Drake's been cleared to play." Ford looks at me and cringes. "Who knows who Coach will play on the starting line, but I wanted to prepare you. I think he was gonna tell you today anyway."

Warner gives me a look filled with pity.

Kane shrugs as though there's nothing I can do.

I knew it was coming. And surprisingly, I'm pretty okay with it. I did my part when I was called up. Hopefully that will mean more opportunities for me in the future.

"Thanks for letting me know." I nod.

"Anytime. Shit, Warner, your line's moving." Ford points.

I chuckle because the line never moved.

Warner scrambles to get up from the white plastic chair and looks closer at the line, then he turns and narrows his eyes at Ford. "Asshole."

Ford laughs and walks away, probably to go find Lena.

That leaves me alone with Warner and Kane. "You two act like brothers."

Warner nods. "Yeah, I guess we were more like brothers than best friends back in the day. Kinda just picked up where we left off."

The smile on his face is a nice change from when they hated one another. It made the locker room tense and being on the ice with them sucked. Thankfully I wasn't on their line, but I saw how frustrated Drake was that they couldn't play nice together. In truth, the fact that Ford wouldn't pass the puck to Warner unless he absolutely had to could be some of what's kept us out of the playoffs. I'm doubtful we'll make it at this point.

"Any more thoughts of retiring?" I ask Kane.

"What?"

We all look behind us to find Jana.

Kane blows out a breath. "Don't get too excited. Nothing's for sure."

"Can I speak to you for a moment?" Jana asks him.

I mouth sorry as he stands and follows her to the front of the boat. Just then, another boat rushes close to ours. There's a cameraman on board with a long lens.

Warner lifts his beer at him.

"How do these motherfuckers sleep at night?" I ask.

"Relax, Jana probably hired these ones."

I watch as the boat goes ahead of our boat, since we're anchored, and snaps a few pictures of Jana and Kane. She waves them off and leans over the boat.

"Not me, idiot, all of them." She points toward where everyone else is. Then she deserts Kane and directs everyone where to go.

Ande comes over to me. "I'm supposed to sit on your lap," she says with raised eyebrows.

I smile and tap my lap.

"Warner! Come here!" Jana yells.

"Watch my line and let me know if anything bites." His face is dead serious.

"I will."

Just as I think Ande is going to sit in my lap, she bypasses me and sits in Warner's now-vacant chair.

"Are you having fun?" I ask.

"Honestly, I'm feeling kind of nauseous," she says and puts her hand on her stomach.

"Seasick?"

"I've never had it before, so I'm not sure if it was the mimosas or the breakfast, but they're not sitting right."

I run my hand over her back. "Want me to see if we can get back to land somehow?"

She shakes her head. "I don't want a picture taken of me leaving this boat. What would they say?"

"Who gives a shit what *they'd* say?" I open my arms. "C'mere. Let me comfort you a little."

Reluctancy is written all over her face, but she does stand and come nuzzle into my lap, placing her head on my shoulder.

I run my hand up and down her back, casting small kisses on the top of her head. "I bet the captain has something that could help."

"I don't want to move right now."

A contented sigh leaves my lips. "Okay. We don't have to go anywhere."

We stay like that for a while longer, and part of me wonders if she falls asleep. That guy on the other boat comes by again, clicking away with his camera, but this is what Jana wants and I'm not opposed to people knowing I'm falling in love with this girl.

After twenty minutes or so, Ande bolts up. "Oh my god!"

She bends over the edge of the boat, throwing up. I hurry and grab her long hair, telling her all will be okay. When she stops vomiting, she remains leaned over the side, mumbling about how embarrassing this is, especially with the other boat there. I reassure her it's fine.

"Oh shit." Ford comes over. "Hold on, I can get you something."

He disappears and Ande takes a break from throwing up for a moment. Her face is pale and clammy when Ford returns with Lena. Is she the something?

"Being seasick is the worst." Lena digs into her purse and pulls out a small pill. "It might not take effect right away and it's probably gonna make you really tired, but it's better than throwing up all day."

Ande doesn't ask any questions and takes the pill.

"Let it dissolve under your tongue," Lena says.

Then Saige comes by with a washcloth and presses it to Ande's forehead. I want to tell them to stop crowding us, that it's my responsibility to take care of her, but it's also nice to see how accepted she's been by all the significant others.

"I thought it was going to be me." Imogen hands Ande a water. "Slow sips."

Ande's face is beet red from all the attention, but she doesn't fight anyone, not even me.

"Honey, your pole!" Imogen screams.

Warner hops over a chair and rushes to his pole. He stares for a moment. "Did it really move?" he asks his wife.

"Nope, just joking."

He picks her up and pretends he's going to throw her overboard.

"Fucking family trait, huh?" he says.

She giggles and holds on tight to his neck. He holds her over the water and there isn't one ounce of doubt in Imogen's face that says she's worried he might drop her. And she's right, because he pulls her close to him and he kisses her instead.

That's trust. That's the kind of trust I want Ande to have in me.

CHAPTER 21

"Is that something you'd want?"
—Ande

Ande

I'm packing to spend a long weekend away with Cory during one of his out-of-town stints while I chat with York on speakerphone.

"Seems like our plan is going well. You haven't slept with him yet, have you?"

"No." Although I've had the urge more than once. The more we spend time together, the closer I get to what I was afraid would happen—I'm falling for Cory again. When I'm around him, I forget why I'm so pissed. I forget the plan I set into motion.

"Good. Sex will complicate things. Do you think he loves you? From the pictures, he looks like he might be in love."

I fold a shirt and place it in my suitcase. "I don't know. He says..."

Talking about Cory with my sister is starting to feel uncomfortable. She always asks a million details.

"What?" she prods.

"He says sweet things."

"Yeah, he always told me sweet things too. Probably has a book with all his swoony lines so he doesn't forget them."

I pack up my toiletries in the bathroom and bring them over to my suitcase. I've seen pictures of Cory at five-star resorts and Michelin-starred restaurants after some games. Figuring out what I should pack isn't easy.

"I was wondering if he's reached out to you? Since he'll be in Denver next week."

She's silent for a while and I'm thinking he did reach out and maybe she doesn't want to tell me because she thinks I won't be able to keep up the act.

"He actually didn't," she says.

"Oh."

"But that doesn't mean much. This Jana sounds like she's got him on a tight leash. The Cory I knew would do anything to save his career. That always took center stage in his head."

I don't say anything, rearranging my suitcase because I'm uncomfortable. She's right. Based on all the conversations I've had with Cory, hockey does take priority. But if he really wants me in his life, where do I fall? I guess I could ask him. Although why do I care?

I squeeze my eyes shut in frustration. It's hard to keep my emotions in check, remember what I'm supposed to be feeling and what's real. Lately they feel reversed. "Yeah, Jana's on top of it. She hired that guy to take pictures of us on that boat."

York laughs. "Was it really seasickness? I felt so bad seeing the pictures with Cory holding your hair back and then you in his arms. I could feel how horrible and embarrassed you must have been."

"I don't know what it was. We had mimosas. Maybe it was the alcohol, but... I'm just glad it's over. And I'm happy the blog people were nice about it rather than saying how gross I am or something."

"They've been really supportive of you and Cory. Almost like your cheerleaders, which must make that Jana happy."

I nod, though she can't see me. "It does. That's why she wants me to go to a few away games. Said that will help solidify our relationship. I guess Cory's reputation has really turned around. Amazing how quickly people forget."

"Until we out that he slept with two sisters." I don't miss the glee in her voice.

"And he's heartbroken like he's left so many others," I add, my voice having far less enthusiasm than hers.

"Of course, that too. I can't wait to see his face when he sees me standing next to you."

York has that vindictive tone she used when Dad told us our mom reached out and wanted to take us to dinner long after she left. York would have no part of it, but I went. In the end, I'd wished I was more like York because my mom said she wanted to be a part of our lives again but never reached out after that.

My phone buzzes. "Gotta go, York, my Uber is here."

"Okay, remember, *do not* sleep with him. I know you, and if you do, those feelings you had for him will come snowballing back."

I zip my suitcase. "Don't worry. I have my own room and stuff."

"I always worry about you, Ande. You're my sister."

My heart melts from hearing her say that. York isn't the heart-to-heart type of woman. She rarely says anything about emotions. The crazy part about this whole charade is how much closer I feel toward her now. And I like it. After Dad died, I felt as if I had no family. I spent the holidays with my friends and there was always an underlying sadness because I didn't share blood with any of them.

"Hey, maybe we can do something for Thanksgiving or Christmas together this year?" I ask before I hang up.

"I'd love to. Mark it on the calendar."

Although the holidays are far away, I love that she committed so quickly. Maybe I'm not the only one who regrets that we weren't close.

We say goodbye and I rush out the door with my suitcase in hand. The team already flew out this morning so they could practice before the game.

I inhale a deep breath as the Uber pulls away from my house and heads toward the highway. With any luck, this might be the last thing I have to do with Cory before we come clean. Four days. I can do this. I can make him fall in love with me, then I'm done.

SAIGE AND TEDI are at the game like Jana promised. Our seats are close to the Fury bench and the sin bin. It's clear why Saige made the trip—Aiden is back on the ice and in the starting line again, which means Cory is back on the second line with Tweetie. Tweetie got knocked down when Warner started the team, but I've never detected any hard feelings between them.

The minute they announce Aiden, Saige stands and cheers. Although I'm happy for them, seeing Cory on the bench breaks me.

"It sucks, right?" Tedi whispers. "I never thought I was this empathetic until I became the girlfriend of a hockey player. Tweetie is better now, but at first, he took it hard."

I nod. "Of course Aiden got his spot back. He should."

Saige sits and glances over, clearly guessing what we're talking about. "I'm sorry," she says with genuine compassion.

"You do not need to apologize. I'm sure Aiden is ecstatic to be back on the ice."

She smiles wide. "Yeah, we've had some tough nights. Let's just hope he's back on his game."

Which he is, because he scores the first goal of the game, solidifying his spot on the team. Aiden must've had a fire under his ass because between him, Ford, and Warner, we're ahead three nothing by the third period. At least that means that Cory's line gets a little extra time on the ice. As if he's got something to prove, Tweetie and Cory do some sort of play that gets the Fury two more goals by the time the game ends. We all cheer when they win five to nothing.

"Truthfully, St. Louis is struggling this year, but a win's a win!" Tedi claps while we head up the stairs.

"Stop putting a damper on the win." Saige lightly shoves Tedi, then comes alongside me. "You know, I'm not just trying to sell my services, but Cory really needs someone to handle his social media. There are some nasty comments on his accounts. I'm not sure he's done anything with them since he joined the team. Maybe you're up for doing it for him?"

I chuckle and shake my head. "No."

"Can you bring it up to him? I never want to put them in an uncomfortable situation." She hands me her card.

"Thanks, Saige. I'll bring it up to him." I take the card. Now more than ever, I want to look up his social media. I don't know how I've managed to resist thus far. When we were apart, I thought it would just make me miserable. Now that we're together, I'm afraid of what comments I might find. "I'm surprised Jana never said anything."

"Cory probably didn't need someone to manage his accounts before, but since he took Aiden's spot for a while, his name is more well known. A few pictures of you two on there wouldn't hurt." She smiles and catches up to Tedi.

I walk behind them, pocketing Saige's card and

processing all the different things that factor into the life of a professional athlete. It's not just playing the game. The job takes over their entire lives.

An average person can leave their job and go out to dinner. They can be rude or tell off a waiter. They can sleep with as many people as they want, and no one cares. But a hockey player only has privacy at home. That's gotta be hard.

"Let's go celebrate!" Tweetie says when he and Cory come out of the locker rooms.

Cory puts his arm around my shoulder. "Sorry, we've got plans. See you guys tomorrow."

"Hey, Jet!" Aiden yells, and Cory turns around. "You did amazing out there. That new play—"

Cory cuts him off. "Thanks. You did too."

Then Cory's escorting me into a taxi, and once we're in the back seat, he gives the driver the name of the hotel.

"Do you mind room service?" Cory asks. "I promise to keep my hands to myself, I just don't feel like being out right now."

I grab his hand and link our fingers, sensing he needs physical comfort of some kind. "Sure."

Cory is quiet most of the ride to the hotel, and we opt for my room since he shares his with Warner. He kicks off his shoes and takes off his suit jacket. I hand him the menu as he sits in the chair in the desk area.

We get our food order, but Cory barely touches his. I try to start a few different conversations, but he's abnormally in his head. I even ask if he wants to talk about anything that's bothering him, to which he says no. He apologizes profusely about his mood and says maybe he should just go back to his room.

Finally, after two drinks from the minibar, he lets it all

out. "I knew Drake was coming back, that the position is his and I was just filling in, but it sucks. I thought I was cool with it, but I didn't realize how much I liked being on the starting line until I wasn't."

I pat the spot next to me on the bed, and he stands from the office chair and sits next to me. The mattress dips from his weight. I get on my knees behind him, massaging his shoulders. He undoes the buttons at the top of his shirt.

"I'm really sorry you have to deal with this." I dig my hands into his shoulders.

"I keep thinking how it'll be years before Drake retires... am I better off trying to score a trade to a different team that doesn't have a great center?"

My hands pause as I think about what it would mean for me if he left the Florida Fury. Which tells me I'm in more trouble than I thought, because I shouldn't care. I definitely shouldn't feel as if there's a weight dragging me down.

"Is that something you'd want?" My voice cracks.

Cory turns around and tugs me into his lap. I get lost in his dark eyes because they're always the best way to tell what he's feeling. I know before he answers that he doesn't want to leave Florida. "No. Maybe if you weren't there, but as things stand right now, I don't want to leave."

I want to tell him to call his agent and look at other teams. I want to tell him that I'm about to break his heart, so he should do what he has to do to be happy, but I say nothing. Truth is, a large part of me doesn't want him to leave. Just the thought of this ending between us feels like a nail piercing my heart. And I really need to get over that feeling because York and I are going to out ourselves soon and then this will all be over, and Cory will hate me.

I open my mouth to tell him the truth, but the energy in the room shifts and his gaze falls to my lips. I inhale, my tongue sliding out to lick my lips. He dips his head down and his fingers thread through the hair on the side of my head. Am I really going to let him kiss me? He's patient and waiting for me to meet him halfway because I've been the one keeping us from having any physical intimacy. Without thinking of the repercussions, I bring my lips to his and immediately know that I don't regret a thing.

CHAPTER 22

"Yes, Cory, back to the hotel."
—Ande

Cory

Having Ande traveling with me is better than I hoped. Now that we're in Chicago and we have a little more free time, I want to take her on a real date. Especially since I ruined the other night with my "poor me" act.

We won against Chicago, although it was a bigger challenge than the last game. Aiden got the game-winning goal. I can't deny that he deserves his position, but being second in line sucks all the same. And Aiden isn't close to retirement like Kane.

I push all the pressure of that aside and knock on Ande's hotel room door. She answers wearing a blue dress that clings to every curve of her body. Her high heels bring her closer to my height. Since she allowed me to kiss her last night, I plan on kissing her more tonight, so the heels will give my neck a break.

"You're leaving me breathless in that dress."

Her cheeks color and she fidgets for a second. "Thank you. I wasn't sure where we were going."

I'm still dressed in my suit from the game because I plan to take her to a nice restaurant and a walk along the Chicago River if it's not too cold. "Feel free to wear this dress to the supermarket anytime with me."

My comment makes her laugh. I love hearing her laugh. It's a boost to the ego to be the one who makes her happy.

"Let's go," she says and steps into the hallway.

I back her up against the wall and place one hand over her head and the other on her hip. "I know you're wearing lipstick, so I apologize ahead of time."

I press my lips to hers. A small moan slips from her throat and I lock her to the wall with my hips, wishing we could do room service and lie naked in bed all night.

She closes the kiss and I honor her wishes, backing off. "Damn, one taste and I'm already hard."

She laughs and touches her lips with her fingertips. "How bad is my lipstick?" She brings her hand to my lips and uses her thumb to wipe. "Because it looks like you're probably wearing more than me."

We go back into her room, where she quickly reapplies her lipstick and I use a tissue to wipe mine clean.

On the way to the elevator, I say, "Feel free to not wear lipstick in the future."

The elevator doors open to the lobby as she laughs with her head tilted back. A guy with a camera is there and snaps a picture, which sobers her up.

She looks at me. "Is this a Jana thing?"

I shake my head, taking her hand and leading her out of the elevator, ignoring the cameraman who follows us, asking me questions about my teammates, how I feel about losing my spot on the first line. I ignore it somehow. My dad taught me a long time ago how to manage my anger. A hot head isn't what any team wants.

Luckily, the doorman sees me coming and opens the car door for us to slide in and he shuts it immediately. I'll have to give him a heavy tip later.

Once we're behind the tinted windows of the black SUV, I say, "I'm sorry."

"It's okay. I'm surprised I'm not used to it. It's like just as we're having a private moment—bam, reality." She crosses her legs, and the slit of her dress opens wider, making me have to adjust myself in my pants. I want those long legs wrapped around me.

"I'm hoping the restaurant offers us more privacy. There were no private rooms, but they promised me no one would bother us." I really hope that's the truth. Ford said he knows the restaurant, and they really do keep their clientele discreet.

We're quiet during the drive and I can't help but wonder where her head is at since mine is on the fact that I want us to spend the night together. I want to dissolve that wall of hers for good so I can see where we stand. If I'm wasting my time here, then maybe I need to speak to my agent about switching teams so I can at least progress in my hockey career.

The SUV parks at the curb and a valet opens the door. I step out first, then turn and hold my hand out for Ande. I swear even the valet sighs at the sight of her legs.

She's all mine, buddy.

We're seated immediately and they tuck us into a corner that feels secluded from most of the other tables. I've never taken Ande to this fancy of a restaurant before, mostly because it's not really me. Sure, for special occasions, but I'm not Ford. He likes this kind of thing for everyday meals, and if he's making reservations for the team, we always end up somewhere like this. But I wanted to do something special for Ande.

Ande picks up a menu and her eyes widen. "Cory, everything is so expensive," she whispers.

"Order what you want."

"But—"

I shake my head. "I appreciate the concern, but I can afford it."

"It doesn't mean you have to spend it. I'd be just as happy at the hot dog place people brag about here. Or pizza? Isn't Chicago known for their pizza?"

I smirk, shaking my head. "This is where we're eating. Pick anything you want."

She sighs and looks over the menu again. "I should pay my share."

"Do you want to know how much the contract I signed was when I got drafted? Would that make you feel better?"

"*No!*" she whisper-shouts. "I mean, that's none of my business."

"Then order something to eat or I'll order for you."

"Fine, bossy pants." She puts down the menu. "Tilapia."

"I was going to get the tilapia. You up for sharing if I get a shrimp pasta instead?"

"Share the meal?" she asks, and I prepare for her to say no. "Sounds good."

"Great." I smile at her.

I order us a bottle of white wine, and we each order a meal, saying we're going to share. While we wait for the food, we talk about the game tonight.

"I'm sorry about being a downer the other night." I know I owe her an apology.

She shakes her head. "No need to apologize. I felt bad for you."

I rock my head back. "Oh shit, a pity party. You can't feel that bad for me. Most guys would kill to do what I do."

She takes my hand, and I open my palm so we can link our fingers. "First of all, I *can* feel bad for you. I can empathize with what you're going through. And yeah, a lot of guys would love to be in your position, but I'm assuming anyone playing professional sports is probably supercompetitive and wants to be the go-to guy."

I huff because of course she gets it. "I did love that last part of the night though."

She smiles and it makes her eyes sparkle a bit in the glow of the candle on our table. "I did too."

Our conversation flows easily while we eat, splitting our meals like a real couple, and I love every minute of it.

After swallowing a mouthful, I say, "I have something to admit."

"What's that?" she asks, wiping her mouth with her napkin.

"I've never had a girlfriend. Never been serious with anyone."

Her smile dims a bit, and my chest constricts.

"But I want you to be my girlfriend. Does that sound too much like what some kid in high school would say?" After the words come out of my mouth, I feel embarrassed. But I want a label on whatever we are.

"Girlfriend? Meaning?" She moves the asparagus around her plate, not looking me in the eyes.

"We're already monogamous, so I guess whatever girlfriend means to you. For me, that means you get a permanent seat in the stands whenever you want to come to a game, but now you have to wear stuff with my number on it. I think I'm promised at least one night during the weekend for a date and maybe a couple times during the week."

"Oh." She nods a few times. "And I would get flowers?" She smirks.

I nod. "Done."

"And would I get to cook you dinner?"

"As long as I get to cook you dinner."

"I could get used to that." She grins.

"We could have sleepovers…"

She chuckles.

I stretch my arms out with my palms up and she places her hands on mine. "So what do you say, Ande? Can we make this official?"

"Yeah," she says in a soft voice.

It's like a bucket of euphoria is dumped over my head, I'm so damn happy. "Then it's official, you're my girlfriend."

She laughs.

"What?"

"It seems like a ridiculous conversation, but I guess in your position, it has to be stated outright." She picks up her fork and eats the shrimp pasta.

"I just want you to know how much I want this. Ande, you grabbed my attention that day on the bus and you've never left my mind since. I want more for us. I want lazy Sundays where we go get coffee. I want pizza and movie nights. I want to rub your feet after a long day. In the end, I just want you."

She inhales and I swear there are tears in her eyes. "You're sure?"

I hold her gaze. "I've never been surer of anything."

A smile creases her lips and it's contagious because my smile could light up the entire room.

"Okay then. But first I really have to tell you something." I don't miss the way her hands grip her cutlery a little tighter when she says that.

The waitress comes over and I ask for two pieces of cheesecake to go. I want to be alone with Ande now. I want to kiss her and hold her and touch her in all the ways that show her she's important to me.

Once the waitress leaves, I look back at Ande. "What did you want to tell me?"

She stares at me for a long time and the longer it takes for her to speak, the more worried I become. She shakes her head. "I was going to suggest the cheesecake thing too. I want to feed it to you this time."

And now I'm hard. "We can feed each other."

I look around for the waitress because I want the check pronto, but the problem with fancy restaurants is they think you want to extend the experience when you really just want to get your girlfriend back to your hotel to strip her naked.

"Sounds good," she says and finishes her glass of wine.

When the waitress does return, I pay the bill and grab the bag with the cheesecake, putting my hand on Ande's back to lead her out of the restaurant. We get a few looks and I have no idea if it's because we're an interracial couple or if they recognize me, but I'm not gonna let them ruin my night. All I see in my immediate future is Ande.

Once we're outside, the night air is a little chilly since it's springtime in Chicago and pretty late at night. "Do you want to walk or—"

"Or," she answers immediately.

"Back to the hotel?"

She laughs. "Yes, Cory, back to the hotel."

She doesn't have to tell me twice. Our car arrives and Ande slides in, me right next to her. My hand lands on her thigh and I trail my fingers up the slit in her dress. She doesn't stop me, so I graze my knuckles over her silk panties. She wiggles in the seat, and I tease her, never going any further because I definitely want to take my time with her tonight.

Once we arrive at the hotel, I take her hand and we

breeze by the few cameramen who must've heard this is where the Fury are staying. We walk by the bar, and of course, all the guys are in there. When they see us, they start shouting, calling us over.

I wave and continue to the elevator. Once the doors shut, the bag of cheesecake drops from my hand and I cage Ande against the wall, smashing my lips to hers. Pure sweetness. That's what Ande is, and I'm lost in her Candy Land.

CHAPTER 23

Andie

God, the kiss we shared last night was like a trial run compared to this. Cory has me locked to the wall of the elevator with his hips. His hardened length presses against my stomach.

"I love you in these heels," he whispers.

His lips explore my jawline and up my ear, where he nibbles on the lobe. His deep breaths send goose bumps over my skin. Then his lips are back on mine, his tongue slipping into my mouth. He groans and his fingers dig into my waist as if he's afraid I'm going somewhere. Our tongues stroke one another's like a soft caress.

Then the elevator door dings and the doors slide open.

"Come on," he says, tugging my hand, but I grab the cheesecake.

"For later."

He stops me in the hall and kisses me briefly. "God, you're fucking perfect."

I laugh until we reach my room, where I dig in my purse to find the key card. Once I retrieve it, I hold it up like a prize and Cory takes it from my hands, sliding it over the pad.

Once we're in the room, I put the cheesecake inside the fridge. Cory takes the opportunity to wrap his arm around my waist and pull me flush against him, his mouth finding the side of my neck.

"I can't wait to see you out of this dress," he whispers.

"Then unzip it."

I push all the shit with York out of my head because this feels too good to second-guess right now. Even if Cory is using me, I'm letting him because I forgot how amazing it feels to be with him like this. How attentive he is and concerned about me giving me exactly what I need.

He slowly unzips the zipper, and the sound is loud in the quiet room, amping up the tension between my legs. His hand slides the fabric off my right shoulder and his lips follow along, then he mimics the same movement on the other side. My dress off my chest, hangs at my hips. It's so formfitting it'll need an extra push to reach the floor. But Cory doesn't worry about that right away. Instead, he reaches around me, and I let my head drop back and rest on his shoulder.

He drags his lips across the skin of my shoulders and his hands each take the weight of one lace-clad breast, his thumbs rubbing over my peaked nipples. He's rock hard behind me, digging into my upper ass. The feel of him drenches my panties even more.

I look up and see that we're in front of the mirror. His eyes shimmer with mischief as he unhooks my strapless bra, letting it free-fall to the carpeted floor.

"Are you sure?" he asks in a low, rough voice. "You want this?"

I nod, watching in the mirror as he continues to undress me. His fingers dig into the side of the dress and push the fabric down my hips and thighs, allowing the fabric to fall to my ankles.

I move to step out of my heels, but he stills my body with his hands. "Uh-uh. Not yet."

He watches me through the mirror, the two of us together. His darker skin is a contrast to my paleness, and although we look more like opposites, we fit perfectly. I've never felt for anyone what I do for Cory. What I see reflected back at me proves what I've felt every day since we've been back together, what I've been trying so hard to deny. This is a man who would do anything for me.

"I think it's your turn," I say, and he chuckles, shrugging out of his suit coat and tossing it on a chair. He toes out of his shoes, but it barely makes a difference in our heights. I swivel around and my fingers fumble with the buttons on his shirt. "I want to undress you."

He positions me to sit on the table over the mini-fridge, and I unbutton his dress shirt, pushing the fabric over his shoulders and down his arms. He unbuttons the shirt at his wrists, allowing me to run my hands over his chiseled chest. With my fingertips, I trace the two wings on either side of his pecs and the scripture on the side of his ribs. I want to know the story behind these works of art, want to know what they mean, but that can wait for another time.

Cory runs his thumb along my lips, and I stare into his eyes. My insecurity tries to rear its head, but the other side of me is stronger now, seeing the emotions in Cory's beautiful eyes.

My fingers fiddle with his belt, then his button, and I lower his zipper, allowing the slacks to fall to the floor and leaving him in a pair of boxer briefs that do little to disguise the hard girth pressing against the fabric from underneath.

I stare at the man in front of me. He's strong and beautiful in both physicality and heart.

"You like what you see?" His voice is hoarse and quiet. As if he'd have any reason to be insecure.

I wind my legs around his, pulling him toward me. He comes easily and his hands land on my ass, pulling me up so my legs wrap around his waist. Backing up, he sits on the edge of the bed, keeping me on his lap.

I can't help but rock along his cock as he palms my breasts, bending down to take one in his hot, wet mouth. I whimper from the sensation that rushes through my body.

"I want you. I need you," I whisper, and he lifts his head and chuckles into my throat.

"In due time, beautiful," he says softly and turns us around, laying me on the mattress. "I don't want to rush this."

I watch him strip off his boxers, his cock bobbing out over the dusting of dark hair on his lower stomach. The sight of it makes my mouth water. He crawls up the bed, hooks his fingers on either side of my panties, and drags them down my legs.

"Have I told you how much I love these legs?" He holds one up and casts kisses all the way up until his hot breath blows on my center.

When the tip of his tongue touches my clit, my head falls to the bed.

"You taste exactly how I remember," he murmurs between my legs.

The man has to have taken a class on going down on a woman because in no time at all, I'm clenching and trying to hold my orgasm at bay as he licks, sucks, and blows on my sensitive nub. Just when I'm writhing under him, he pushes two fingers inside me, arching up, and presses on my lower stomach at the same time.

His name leaves my lips like a plea for mercy because it

feels as though I'm about to explode out of my own body. I ride his fingers as his mouth assaults my clit in the best possible way. "I'm going to come. I don't want to come yet. I want you to do this again and again."

He thrusts the fingers in and out of me, and the slick sound of my desire echoes through the room. "I promise there's gonna be so much more. I'll never get enough of how you taste."

And that's all it takes for my eyes to roll back as the orgasm takes over. I arch up off the bed, but he keeps my hips in place and slows his movements, allowing me to come in waves until my body relaxes. Afterward, he slowly draws his fingers from my pussy and licks them clean, still watching me.

Seriously, who made this man?

He leaves the bed and digs into his slacks, returning with a condom. I watch with rapt attention as he rests his knees on the mattress and runs the condom down his thick shaft.

Running the tip of his dick along my folds, he wets himself before pushing the tip in. "You're soaked. Is that all for me, beautiful?"

"Yes!" I sound a tad excited, but he inches inside me, holding his weight so he's just above me.

His arms settle on either side of my head and I stare into his eyes while he slowly sinks into me, holding still at first. He stretches me in the best way and my back arches, my fingers digging into his strong shoulders until he finally withdraws and thrusts back inside me.

I clench around his length, and he stares down at me with hooded eyes. He rocks his hips back and forward in a perfect cadence that makes me moan and whisper inaudible words of praise. When he fucks me hard, his pelvis hits my clit and a million nerve endings go into a frenzy, begging for more of him.

He's quick to take one of my legs and rest the back of it on his chest, drilling deeper inside me. His rhythm is perfect, as if he practices it as much as he does circling the net before tapping in a goal. Cory knows how to get a woman off and I push the reasons to why that could be out of my head, willing to just enjoy this man who wants to satisfy his girlfriend.

He feeds off my sounds and does this surprising circle of his hips then thrusts his pelvis to hit my clit, over and over again, torturing me, making me beg for release. He keeps on doing it, almost making me mad. I desperately want to come, but I need this one to count, so I clench as hard as I can, but all the exercises in the world are no match for Cory and his magic dick.

He works my body until my orgasm presses against every cell in my body and I have no control. I explode and scream his name as my body feels as if I'm floating on air.

I struggle to find my breath after. I've never come that hard. Maybe it's because of all the lead-up. We've been dating and doing little to no touching. Every night he dropped me off, I'd dig out my favorite toy and use my imagination, but it didn't do an ounce of justice to what it's like to have Cory Freeman in the flesh.

All my nerve endings are on high alert, but he rides me, thrusting over and over again. Telling me sweet things and dirty things and grabbing one breast, squeezing it as I arch my back like an offering. A growl comes out of him, and he stills inside me, his dick twitching and pumping out his release. I relax into the mattress like a splayed jellyfish.

"Damn, Ande, I think I blacked out. That pussy is gold,

woman." He climbs off the bed, and I make sure to check out his amazing ass on his way to the bathroom.

I hear the toilet flush, then the faucet running. He returns with a washcloth in his hands and I can't help staring at his dick swinging between his legs on his way back.

"Keep staring and round two will start sooner than you think."

He passes me the washcloth and I clean up, handing it back. He tosses it over his shoulder, unconcerned and climbs into bed with me, takes me in his arms, and kisses me. Not a quick peck like he's thanking me for the lay. His tongue is languid and unhurried. His thumb runs up and down along my cheek and he tucks my body as close to his as it can get.

It's then that I know the game is over. I'm going to break both of our hearts.

CHAPTER 24

"I will never regret anything about us."

Cory

It's pretty clear that the Florida Fury won't be winning the Cup this year. We all knew it, but now it's for sure. I care, I really do, but I'm enjoying Ande so much that it's hard to be upset.

Like right now, she's giving me an unapologetic blow job. How can I be upset?

The minute I walked into her house, she kissed me and undid my pants, falling to her knees.

Watching my cock move in and out of her mouth makes me see stars. Her eyes stay steadily on me while her hot, wet mouth works me. She's perfected her method from the way she uses her tongue to leave wetness along my length and twist around the head of my dick. And she actually takes me down her throat until she can't handle anymore, then she sucks the living shit out of me while she gets air again.

She has lipstick on, so it's leaving residue on my dick that I don't think I'm going to bother wiping off because it's hot as fuck. I want to remember this moment again tonight and jerk off to it.

The best part about Ande giving me head is that she enjoys it. Small moans escape her mouth, and she worships my dick—sucking and licking and kissing my cock until my head hits the door behind us.

She doesn't even flinch when I grab a handful of her hair and rock my hips, thrusting into her mouth. My balls tense and my orgasm comes in record time.

I still her with my hand in her hair as my orgasm hits me full force and I flood her mouth. My dick pulses and twitches until the last drop, then she swallows. She always fucking swallows. Afterward, I groan as I watch her clean me up with her tongue.

"God, Ande, I fucking love you."

She pauses and I realize what I said, clearing my throat.

She quickly stands and goes to her kitchen sink, washing her hands.

I zip my pants back up and follow her into the kitchen. "Listen, I—"

She shakes her head. "No. It's fine. Just one of those things that comes out. No biggie."

I hand her a towel to dry her hands. "It wasn't the blow job or the orgasm that made me say it. It's the truth. I love you, Ande. But if you're not ready to tell me you feel the same, that's okay, but you should know that's where I stand."

Her breath shudders and she looks at me. Her mouth opens and she closes it again.

"This is shit timing to tell you this, but Tedi and Tweetie are waiting in the car outside." I cringe. We're all going bowling tonight.

Her eyes grow wide. "What? I thought we were meeting them?"

"You know Tweetie. I called him and he's like, 'We got an Uber SUV, so we'll just swing by,' and well... here we are."

She playfully slaps me. "You let me give you head when our friends are outside waiting?"

I laugh. "Hate to break it to you, beautiful, but I'm not gonna turn down a blow job from the woman I adore. Ever."

Ande gives me a coy smile. "Let me grab my stuff." She walks by me to head to her bedroom.

I love that she refers to my teammates and their wives and girlfriends as *our* friends now. Because our lives really have merged together. And I have fallen in love with her. I'm pretty sure she has too, but she might need more time to admit it, even to herself, so I'll give it to her.

She comes out of her bedroom wearing fresh lipstick and a cross-body purse with a strap that falls right between her breasts. I love those things.

Remembering the look on her face when she was speechless moments ago, I ask, "Was there something you wanted to tell me?" I reach for the door handle.

She's quick to shake her head. "No. We can talk later. We don't want to make Tedi and Tweetie wait any longer."

"Good thing I came so quick." I wink and she giggles as I open the door.

"Good thing I give such spectacular head."

Now I'm the one laughing.

She steps out and I follow, then she locks up her place.

"Are Trevor and Gregg coming?" I ask on the walk to the car.

"Yeah, they're meeting us there."

"Perfect." I open the car door for her to find Tweetie and Tedi making out. At least they're not pissed I took so long.

We situate ourselves in the SUV, us in the third row and Tweetie and Tedi in the second. Ande's hand is secure in mine, and I say a small prayer that telling her I love her doesn't scare her off. But I've always worn my feelings on my sleeve with her and I don't want to change that now.

WE PUT Ford and Warner on the same team because at this point, I think we're all sick of them competing over every little thing. It turns out they're actually worse when they're on the same team than when they're competing against each other.

They high-five when Warner gets his second strike in a row.

"Suck that, boys," Ford says.

We shake our heads.

Lena comes to sit in our area. "I'm with you guys now."

We all laugh and welcome her to the team.

It's Ande's turn and I've decided I love bowling. It gives me the opportunity to stare unabashedly at her ass as she takes her turn. She's a horrible bowler. Not that I'm much better. We both suck and are keeping Tweetie and Tedi from winning.

"Where's Kane?" someone asks.

"He said he was staying at home," I say.

In reality, he told me he needs some alone time to come to terms with what he wants to do next season. We still have some games this season, but none of them really count.

"Do you think he'll really retire?" Tedi asks in a low voice.

All the guys shrug.

"I wish he wouldn't. He still stopped how many goals this year?" Aiden says.

Ever since Ande and I got closer, I haven't considered trying for a trade to another team. I'm not even sure the Gerhardts would consider it, but I'm happy here and I'm not sure our relationship could handle long distance. Nor do I want that kind of relationship with this woman anyway.

The pitchers of beer flow and we order appetizers,

which means greasy food. None of us will be in any condition to play the day after tomorrow.

Ande sits on my lap after taking one pin down on the second try. "I suck."

I put my lips at her ear. "You're the best sucker, beautiful. I can't wait for you to suck again."

Her cheeks turn red, and I want to drag her to a bathroom and fuck her against a wall. But we're doing so well with the "fans" that I don't want to fuck it up. They'd probably miss the fact it was Ande and say I was cheating on her or some shit or try to slut shame her for getting it on in a public bathroom. Like a committed woman can't get freaky at a bowling alley.

"Well, you're a pretty fantastic licker," she says and pulls me in for a kiss that's heavier and longer than either of us expects. But her blow job was like an appetizer before the main course, and I had to leave before I got my full meal.

Ford and Warner win, much to their excitement and our dismay.

We decide to leave the bowling alley when blacklight bowling starts, since there are a lot of families. Tweetie says he knows a bar down the road we can walk to.

All of us head down the street. Maybe a few of us can get by without being recognized, but with all of us together, it's impossible. We get stopped three times by different women —who all want to talk to our significant others more than us.

I'm talking to Drake when I overhear a woman ask Ande, "Do you really believe him?"

I want to intervene, but I also want to hear the answer.

"What do you mean?" she asks, still being polite.

Another woman is cooing to Lena about Annabelle, and

one woman reaches to touch Imogen's stomach and she steps back and politely declines her.

"I mean, does a playboy really change his spots?" the woman asks and looks at me, her eyes slowly moving up and down my body. Oh, this isn't gonna be good.

"Um..." Ande seems tongue-tied. I wish she would just stick up for us. "I think they can." Her voice doesn't have the confidence I hoped it would.

"Ford did. Look at him now," one of her friends says, but the woman isn't going to let it go so easily.

She shrugs. "I guess, but I think Cory is different."

I'm growing more annoyed each time this woman opens her mouth. I turn away to try to compose myself and Drake tells me what they say doesn't matter, but I spot a tattoo shop across the street and an idea forms in my head.

I take Ande's hand. "Want to know how serious I am about Ande?" I interrupt them.

The woman's face flushes as if she didn't know I was listening.

I guide Ande across the street, and everyone follows us to the tattoo parlor. As I open the door, Ande puts on the brakes like a dog who realizes he's standing at the vet doors. She might as well sit down and go limp; I cannot move without dragging her.

"No way. What are you going to do?" she asks.

"I already thought about it before. Now I'm gonna do it." I tug and she tugs back, shaking her head vehemently.

"How romantic," Tedi says. She hits Tweetie. "What about you?"

"I love you, Tedi, but this is other level shit."

"Seriously?" She crosses her arms.

Tweetie gives me a "fuck you" look. I don't want to cause any problems for the other couples, but I do want Ande's name on my skin because I believe in us. I believe we're as permanent as that ink.

Finally moving Ande inside, I go over to the counter. Lucky for us, the guy is a hockey fan.

"You know what? Make that two." Tedi comes up next to me. "You might not believe in us, but I do." She pokes Tweetie in the chest.

"Fuck. Make it three," he says, and Tedi smiles in my direction.

I shake my head. "You guys don't have to."

"Is he really going to do it?" the woman who started this whole thing asks.

Ande comes to my side, her hand pulling down my arm to get my attention. "I can't let you do this," she whispers. "I'm serious."

"Give me one reason. I told you earlier that I love you. No matter what happens, I always want to remember you. I honor people on my skin."

"So, like, you're going to do a symbol or something?" A line forms on the bridge of her nose.

I laugh. "Not a symbol. Your name. Right here." I strip off my shirt and a few women snap some pictures. I roll my eyes while pointing right below my wing where my heart would be. "A heart with your name. Nothing huge."

She blows out a breath. "But it's permanent."

"Technically tattoos can be removed nowadays," Paisley says from behind us.

I give her a death stare, as does Tedi.

"We need to talk," Ande says and pulls my hand.

The technician calls my name.

"Beautiful." I put my hand on her cheek and stare into her eyes. "I love you and I want your name on my skin.

Would you sign your name so that's what I can have tattooed there?"

A strangled cry leaves her throat. "Cory."

"Please."

She inhales deeply. "I really wish you'd listen to me."

"The decision is made." I lower my mouth to hers, casting a brief kiss on her lips. "Come on."

She allows me to lead her over to the station. I tell the tattoo artist that Ande's going to write the heart and her name. I know she doesn't want me to do it, but I think it's because she's not as sure about us as I am. She'll come around, and maybe someday she'll tattoo my name on her. I laugh to myself, not knowing if I'd want ink to tarnish that beautiful skin of hers.

She sits next to me while the tattoo artist prepares the tattoo. After the stencil is on, she tries one last-ditch effort to get me to change my mind. "Isn't there anything temporary? So you can get used to it and see if you really want it? Just for a few weeks or something."

I look at the man who's going to tattoo me. "Go ahead. She's just scared I'm going to regret this." I turn in her direction. "I will never regret anything about us. I love you, Ande."

I squeeze her hand, and the needle buzzes before touching my skin.

She stays by my side the entire time, and I swear I catch a small smile after it's over. I assure myself she just needs a little time to get to the same place I am. That's all.

CHAPTER 25

Ande

It's like déjà vu. I'm back in Jana's office and we're waiting for Cory to join us after practice.

"He got your name tattooed on him. How exciting!" Jana is on cloud fucking cuckooville. She thinks this whole transformation we've made is the best thing ever.

Apparently the women from the other night sent their pictures to one of the blogs. The problem is they pinned me as maybe not as invested in our relationship because I was trying to talk Cory out of the tattoo. I can't handle all this shit anymore. Other people's opinions, the pressure my sister is putting on me, my feelings for Cory, and the guilt that I'm lying to him.

"Not really. There's a lot that can happen. It's not like we're married." I shake my head, knowing the real reason why I hate the tattoo. Because I have to tell Cory soon that I started this thing between us with the goal of hurting him. That I wanted revenge against him sleeping with other women. That he'd convinced me I was special, and I wasn't. That I made him fall in love with me just to pull him down into the trenches with me. And I have no idea how I'm going to do this.

I have to talk to York also. I've been lying to her since I slept with Cory in Chicago. Somewhere during all this, I detoured off the paved path that was our plan and I hopped onto a pebbled dirt road covered in bumps. Things would be going smooth if I'd stuck to the plan and made Cory fall for me and not done the same in return. But I didn't do that, and now I love him.

"It's romantic."

I figure I'll just disagree silently and change the subject. "Have you talked to Kane recently?"

She almost drops her sparkling water but catches it at the last minute. "What? No. Why would you ask that?"

"I was just wondering. I mean, with the Fury not making the playoffs... I didn't know if—"

She perks up in her chair. "Did you hear something? Does Cory know something?"

She looks as frantic as I was the night Cory got the tattoo.

"No." I should probably keep my big mouth shut. "Anyway. Where is Cory?" I tap my glass.

He finally shows up a few minutes later, freshly showered and smelling wonderful. He bends down and kisses me before taking the seat next to me, thigh to thigh, putting his arm around the back of the couch.

"Ah, you two are adorable!" Jana uses her remote to turn off the lights and lower the screen, pulling up that damn blog again. She actually has circles on the chart that shows Cory as the number one–taken hockey player. "Did you know you beat out Ford and Warner this week? That tattoo stint has women swooning for you, Cory Freeman."

She scrolls down, and sure enough, there are even GIFs of Cory in the chair, getting the tattoo. Words like lovesick, devoted, happily ever after are all over the screen.

"But they aren't so sure about you, Ande." She scrolls further and there are some GIFs with my picture. Great.

And the words on the screen now are bitch, undeserving, and cold.

"Wonderful." I look at Cory, whose nostrils are flaring.

"Tell me I can go in and comment," he says, straightening his back and taking my hand. "Shut these women down."

Jana turns everything off with the click of a button and puts up her hand. "I know it's upsetting, but Ande can turn this around."

"I'm not getting a tattoo," I tell her, then guilt carries my gaze to Cory. "No offense."

He laughs and squeezes my hand. "That's okay."

"Don't you think this is getting a little ridiculous?" I ask Jana. All I can think of is the backlash that will come when I break his heart.

"Truthfully, I think the more they see you together, the more they'll come around. There was one awful comment 'You'd think she'd be happier having a hot hockey god tattoo her name on him. Hashtag lucky.' A lot of women just kind of jumped on the bandwagon."

"I don't like them saying those things about Ande. They don't even know her." Cory squeezes my hand.

Now I feel even worse that he's defending me. "It's okay. I'm sure it'll pass. These things have a way of going away." I look to Jana for confirmation.

"Someone else will take the spotlight soon. If only I could manufacture it to be someone else on the Fury." She laughs. "But I really called you both in because the turnaround on this was amazing. You went from douche to relationship god in no time."

Cory stands first. "Thanks, Jana. So it's cool if we're off the radar for a bit?"

She smiles wide. "Yes, now you just reap those rewards

like Ford and Warner. Unless you want to throw a marriage in there? Baby?"

My stomach knots and Jana must see something on my face.

"I'm kidding."

She hugs us each goodbye and we leave her office. We walk hand in hand to the elevator and Cory presses the button. He's telling me about how practice went, how he really enjoys skating with Tweetie and this right-wing guy, Train. They call them T and T. But I'm not really listening because I'm thinking of how to tell him I've been lying. I keep opening my mouth to confess, but nothing comes out.

"Now can we go back to my place so I can have my way with you all night?" He walks me backward until I hit the wall of the elevator, his hand tilting my head up while he bends down to kiss me. It's soft and sweet and loving.

I nod. "I just have to grab some things because I have to be at work early."

"Okay," he says. "I'll stop at the grocery store and pick us up something for dinner."

"Perfect."

We step out to the parking lot, and he kisses me good-bye, telling me he loves me before we part ways. The minute I'm in my vehicle, I dial up York.

"You must have one magic pussy," she answers, instead of saying hello like a normal person.

"What? Why?"

"You know why. He tattooed your name on his heart. That's like romance movie shit, Ande." She must be doing something on the computer because I can hear the click of keystrokes and a mouse.

"I didn't want him to do it, which brings up something I wanted to tell you—"

She cuts me off. "Don't think you've been fooling me. You totally slept with him. There's no way a guy would do that if they weren't getting the goods."

"York..."

She huffs. "How did I taste?" She laughs, but I feel sick from her comment. "Just kidding. Whatever you did doesn't matter. We have him right where we want him. I have a meeting this week, so let's plan on breaking him into pieces next week. Or maybe when they play Denver. Why don't you come out here? That would surprise him more. "

"I'm going to tell him," I blurt.

"What? No, you can't. We planned this already."

"I love him, York."

She screams at the top of her lungs. "You have got to be fucking kidding me!"

"I didn't plan to. I tried not to. But I love him, and he's already going to be so mad at me. I'm just going to tell him tonight. Rip off the Band-Aid. I can't keep this secret anymore."

She scoffs. "He's going to hate you. Kick you out of his life for good."

I turn right to head to Cory's. "Then he hates me, but I can't carry this guilt around anymore. He's been so good to me. I can't keep deceiving him. And I can't publicly hurt him."

"You're such a fool. If you think he's going to forgive you for this, you're wrong. What? Do you think you can live happily ever after like one of those other couples? Don't be a child, Ande."

I knew she wouldn't make this easy. I'd hoped with the way we've grown closer lately that she'd maybe want the best for me. Be able to see past her hurt to see how much he means to me. He's more than proven himself as not being a playboy anymore. I forgive him for sleeping with her that night when I thought we might be starting something.

"I don't know what will happen, but I know I can't do this anymore. I have to tell him." I drive onto his street, and Cory pulls up behind me. What is he doing? "I gotta go. I'll call you after and let you know how it goes." My thumb hovers over the end call button.

"I'm not picking up the pieces of your heart," she says flatly, no emotion.

And here I thought we had grown closer, like sisters.

"I won't call you then. Bye, York."

She hangs up and I sit for a moment until Cory opens up my door.

"What's wrong?" He bends down to my level, swiping a tear from my cheek. "Don't let those stupid people get to you." He stands and holds out his hand.

"I thought you were going to the store?" I sniffle.

He shrugs. "I changed my mind. I just want to be with you. How about we just order Chinese food?"

I rise to my tiptoes and kiss him. "Sounds perfect." I should probably be at my house when I break us. That way it's not awkward, and he can just leave me a crumpled mess on my floor.

"I thought you were going home first before you came here."

I totally forgot when I was on the phone with my sister. It doesn't matter though. Cory won't be asking me to stay the night after I confess the truth anyway.

"I changed my mind too," I say.

I walk through the door and toward the kitchen, but Cory picks me up bridal style and carries me toward the bedroom.

"What are you doing?"

"Having my appetizer," he says and deposits me on the bed. "Is that okay with you?"

What harm could come from one last hookup? I get up on my knees and grab the hem of my shirt, tearing it over my head, then I unbutton my pants.

He crawls up on the bed. "You know I love undressing you."

"I know, but I really want you. I want the outside world to vanish and have it just be me and you." I place my hands on his scruffy cheeks.

He tilts his head and stares at me long and hard. "Do you need to tell me something? You seem really upset. Were you talking to someone on the phone?"

"Just my sister."

"Can't wait to meet her," he says.

My throat closes up and tears burn my eyes. I smash my mouth to his, sliding my tongue into his mouth. I push my body flush against his hard one.

He doesn't ask me why I'm on the brink of losing it. He doesn't ask me anything. He just lowers me to the bed and turns my manic kiss into a slow, measured one. His fingers roam my body, exploring as if it's our first time. We slowly unclothe one another as our lips discover new places to kiss.

I stop him when he goes into the drawer for a condom. "I'm on the pill."

His eyes are unwavering on me. "I'm clean. I've never not used a condom before, and we get a full work up through the team every month."

"I'm clean, too."

He nods, and for the first time, there's nothing between us. It's flesh against flesh as he lowers his body over mine and pushes inside me. His pace is slow and methodical and full of passion. I grip his shoulders, and his hands dig under my ass and raise it off the mattress as he slowly thrusts inside me.

We make love for the first time. At some point, my tears subside, and my moans are the only sound in the room. He watches me the whole time, lowering his mouth to mine, kissing me as slowly as he's entering and leaving me.

"I love you, beautiful," he whispers. "Don't ever leave me. I don't know what I would do."

I cling to him after that because I am going to lose him. This is a goodbye instead of another milestone in our relationship.

I come quietly on a moan, my body stiffening under him. As if he was waiting on me, he comes only seconds after. While he's growing soft inside me, he rises up on his elbows and smiles at me.

"I love you, Cory. So much." Tears prick my eyes.

"Hey, beautiful, that's a good thing." He swipes the tears away.

It won't be once he finds out what I've done. I have to come clean too, but not tonight. Tomorrow I'll force myself to suffer the consequences of my actions.

CHAPTER 26

"Revenge is supposed to be sweet."

Ande

After Cory and I made love, we ordered Chinese food, stayed in bed naked, and made love three more times before finally getting some sleep. By the time I woke in the morning, I had to rush to work. Tonight is the night I tell him. It's their last home game for the season and there's no way I can keep the truth hidden any longer.

I decide I need to talk to someone who will give me the best advice on how to go about telling Cory the truth —Trevor.

"Ande, you have to tell him," Trevor says where I sit next to him in his office.

"I know." I put my head in my hands. "It's just... he's so great. How was I so stupid to think this was a good idea?"

He draws my hands away from my face. "You're human. You're imperfect. You've had experiences that taught you to believe the worst in men."

"Still..."

"What's done is done. Don't beat yourself up. Do I wish you would've come to me sooner so I could talk you out of this? Of course, because honestly, your sister sounds a little toxic." He sighs. "I would've told you that you never could've pulled this off without falling for him. And even if you could, you never would've been able to live with the guilt of purposely hurting someone."

"He's going to hate me."

"Maybe not. He's a great guy. Maybe he'll understand. I mean, he did sleep with your sister."

"Unknowingly."

"But it happened after you had all those other moments together and he made a point of trying to get you back. I can understand why you were hurt and distrustful. I think the two of you just need to sit down and clear it all up."

A knock on Trevor's door pulls our attention to Tabitha, who's holding a box. "Just got this delivered for you by courier." She lingers in the doorway.

"Don't you have work to do?" Trevor asks her, taking the box and shooing her away.

"What if he already found out somehow and it's, like, a horse head or something?"

Trevor's eyebrows shoot up. "Your imagination amazes me sometimes. Open the box, Ande."

I use the scissors on his desk to cut the tape. When I lift the top of the box, I see two tickets to tonight's game. Cory has a thing for real tickets.

I hold them up and Trevor snatches one out of my hand. "I'll take that one."

There's also a jersey. His jersey with a note pinned on it. "Wear me?"

I hold up the note and Trevor smiles. "I guess he's not participating in that competition with the other guys. I wanted you to get some gaudy fifty-cent necklace with his number on it." Trevor laughs.

I roll my eyes. "We're new."

"Well now, you can sleep in his number after it all falls apart."

"Trevor!" I yelp.

He laughs. "Sorry. I'm sure it'll be fine. Listen. I'll go with you. We'll go to Carmelo's afterward, you pull him aside and tell him, and if he's not responsive or he ends it, I'm there to take you home and dry your tears."

I nod. I know I can trust Trevor to be there for me. "Okay."

He puts the jersey in the box, along with one of the tickets, and puts the lid back on. Holding my hands, he says, "You can do this. If he truly loves you, he'll forgive you."

I'm not sure if Trevor is trying to instill hope or if he truly believes it, but I know I have no choice. I have to tell Cory tonight, consequences be damned.

"Okay," I say for the millionth time. "I can do this."

He picks up his ticket. "I'll have to meet you there because I have that meeting at the hookah bar place."

"Oh yeah. I meant to show you what I did on that."

We go back to work, which I'm thankful for because it gets my mind off what I have to do tonight.

But when I leave at five o'clock to go home and get ready, my gut twists, knowing what's coming.

I'M SITTING in my seat at the arena, waiting for Trevor to join me.

"I see someone got some girlfriend wear," Imogen says, smiling at Cory's jersey. "I wonder if they planned it." She takes off her jacket and shows off Warner's jersey, where they've sewn a little number thirty-four over her belly as well. It's too cute.

"How are you feeling?" I ask.

She places her hand on her belly. "I was nervous until I

got through the first trimester, but the doctor says every-thing looks exactly like it should." I see the relief in her eyes.

One by one, each wife or girlfriend shows up wearing their significant other's jersey. We all match.

"Why do you think they did this?" Tedi asks.

"To make us look like idiots," Paisley says.

Jana walks down the stairs. I'm surprised to see her. She usually sits in the suite with her dad and a bunch of other team executives. "What the hell happened? Is this some, 'We wear jerseys on Fridays' thing?" She says it like in the movie *Mean Girls*.

"Something the boys planned." Saige shrugs.

"You know what we should do?" Tedi says. "I say the next time we're all at a game together, none of us wear anything with their number on it. Or maybe we switch it up and we'll wear a different guy's jersey. I'll take Cory's since he tattoos his girlfriend's name on his skin." She reaches out with grabby hands.

I laugh. "Hey, Tweetie got a tattoo for you."

She rolls her eyes. "He got my initials."

"Still..."

"I guess it's something." She turns around.

My phone rings in my pocket. Trevor's name flashes across the screen. "Where are you?"

"I'm trying to find the ticket. I left it on the desk, but I came back to get it and it's not here. Did you take it with you?" I hear him rustling through paper.

"No. I never saw it after you took it from me. Are you sure you didn't tuck it in your pocket or something?"

"I've checked everywhere. Okay, I'm gonna retrace my steps. I'll call you back."

"Let me know. Jana's down here, so maybe I could get her to get you in."

I hang up and Jana glances at me, clearly having heard her name. "What's up?"

"Cory is obsessed with real tickets, so he sent me this jersey and two tickets earlier today. Trevor's supposed to meet me here and he can't find his."

"Tell him to go to will call. I'll call down there now." She picks up her phone and talks to someone for a few minutes, then looks at me and gives me a thumbs-up. "They know to expect him."

That was really nice of her. I hate feeling like a pain, but I need Trevor here tonight.

"Thanks," I say and pick up my phone, but someone sits down in what would be Trevor's seat and I exhale in relief. "Were you playing a joke on me?" I turn to face him.

Except it's not Trevor.

It's York.

"What are you doing here?" I ask.

"We're seeing our plan through," she says smugly. "Did you tell him yet?"

"How did you get this ticket?" I ask.

"I went to your office to talk some sense into you. That receptionist is a dimwit. She actually left me alone. Saw the ticket on your boss's desk when I went to check if he knew where you were and snagged it."

"York!"

"What? You weren't going to give me a ticket."

My phone rings and I answer Trevor's call. "I know what happened, but Jana says go to will call. She put your name in."

"Tabitha just told me your sister came to the office today. Is she there?" Trevor asks.

"Yeah."

"She stole the ticket off my desk?"

"I'm so sorry, Trevor."

"It's not your fault," he says, but I hear the annoyance in his tone.

"Just please hurry," I whisper. "She wants to go through with the plan." I glance at the ice. "Warm-ups are starting. He's gonna see me with her."

"I'm coming," he shouts and hangs up.

"York—" I turn to try to talk to her.

"Who are you?" Tedi asks, being her usual inquisitive self.

"I'm York, Ande's sister." She put her hand out to shake.

Tedi looks at me. "I didn't know you had a sister."

"She likes to keep me a secret." York laughs.

So far it's just the away team on the ice.

"Why don't we go get a snack? A beer? I'm sure after your flight you must be hungry." I stand and wait for her, but York stays in her seat.

"No. I want to see him."

"Cory?" Imogen asks. "Oh, you'll love him. He's so sweet to your sister. She snagged a good one." Imogen is all smiles and pleasantries, but I'm already cringing because I know York won't be the same back.

"A good one, huh?" York says. "You can sit down, Ande, I'm not going anywhere. He's going to come out and see us sitting here together so he knows."

All the girls are obviously confused, whispering to each other with furrowed brows. Does Florida get earthquakes? Because I'd gladly let the earth swallow me whole right now.

"What are we missing?" Tedi is the only one with guts to ask me. She's tried to lower her voice, but York hears her.

"The good guy that you guys all love slept with both me *and* my sister." She sits back and crosses her legs.

I've never seen Tedi speechless, but she is now.

"You knew?" Tedi asks me.

"Not only did she know, but we came up with a plan to get back at that fucker and now he has my sister's name tattooed over his heart. Talk about the best payback ever." York sits back smugly in her seat, and I want to strangle her.

Tedi opens her mouth to say something but quickly shuts it. The girls all whisper with one another and look over their shoulders at York.

The Fury players skate out for warm-ups, and each of the guys looks up at our section as they always do. Imogen blows a kiss to Warner. Lena's late with Annabelle on her hip, but she walks right down to the glass and Ford skates over and places his hand on the glass. Their image is on the Jumbotron and all the early spectators gush over the display. Tweetie thrusts his pelvis toward Tedi, and Maksim nods to Paisley while Aiden smiles wide at Saige and gives her a wink.

And Cory... Cory stares at us slack-jawed. Even after Ford elbows him to go take a shot, he just stares at York and me.

My sister waves dramatically at him.

"Stop it, York," I murmur.

"Oh, come on. Revenge is supposed to be sweet." She keeps her eyes pinned on Cory.

She's wrong. Revenge tastes pretty damn sour right now.

CHAPTER 27

"Then act more sisterly."

Cory

"What the hell?" I say to myself. "Why is York sitting next to Ande and why does Ande look like she wants to throw up?"

"Let's go, Jet." Ford elbows me to start warming up.

"I'm fucked," I say.

He follows my line of vision up to the stands. "Who's the blonde next to Ande?"

"That would be York."

"And who's York? Her sister?"

"Fuck you. No way." I give him a death glare.

Warner skates over and stops. "Coach is gonna have both your asses if you don't warm up. What's going on?" He looks into the stands. "I know, Gen is so fucking adorable. That little thirty-four on the jersey. Too bad Lena's not pregnant." He stares at Ford.

"No, because I have a daughter with her own little jersey with my number on it." Ford rolls his eyes. "And if I go over there and give her attention, you know we'll be on the Jumbotron."

"We should bet to see how many times we get on the Jumbotron next year after my son or daughter is born. Loser pays for vacation at the end of the year." Warner holds out his gloved hand and Ford fist-bumps him, agreeing.

"One day you two are gonna realize you don't have to always one-up the other," I say, still staring at Ande and York.

"Is that Ande's sister?" Warner asks, ignoring me. "I didn't know she has a sister."

I squint. No way is York her sister. But then again, she's sitting in the seat that is supposed to be Trevor's. "No. That's York."

Aiden skates up to get in on the gossip. "And how do we know York?"

"She was my hookup in Denver."

They all crack up laughing.

"You were hooking up with Ande's sister?" Aiden asks.

"She's not her sister. There's no way." I fight what they're saying, but now that they're side by side, I see a resemblance. It's not super obvious, but it's there. Enough that these assholes can see it.

"What if she is though?" Tweetie asks, because of course he wants in on this.

"Hey, assholes, someone shoot a puck!" Kane screams from the net.

"We're busy. See the blonde beside Ande? That's her sister and Jet's former hookup."

I shove Ford. "Fuck no. There's no way it is."

"Wouldn't it be funny if it was?" Tweetie says. "Mr. Romantic who tattoos names over his heart is unknowingly sleeping with two sisters. I'll be boosted up that list in no time and you'll be bumped right off it."

"Okay, Mr. Initials," Warner makes fun of Tweetie.

"And what did you do?" Tweetie taunts him.

"I put a ring on her finger and a baby in her belly," Warner says.

Ford high fives him. "Amen."

"I guess we'll find out after the game how much shit Jet's stepped in," Aiden says, cringing as he skates toward the net.

Everyone else starts their warm-up, but I can't stop looking at Ande. So much so that I'm thankful when warm-ups are done and we go back into the locker room before the game officially starts.

All the players are razzing me, questioning me while I'm on my phone, trying to see if York and Ande are friends on social media.

"Get off your phone, Freeman!" Coach Vittner yells.

I put my phone away and wish my heart would stop racing, but I have no idea what the hell is going on. I have no idea what York might be telling Ande up there.

"Freeman, you're taking first line tonight. We don't need to worry about Drake getting hurt on a game that doesn't count," Coach says.

Aiden glances at the floor. It sucks being friends with someone you compete with for a position. I think he feels guilty.

"Are you sure, Coach? Jet's already gonna take a beating off the ice tonight," Ford says.

All the guys laugh at my expense.

"I don't even want to know what you're talking about, Jacobs." Coach shakes his head. Ford opens his mouth to explain, but Coach ends the conversation. "Go out there and kick ass, boys. Even if the game doesn't mean anything, you have a reputation to protect because next year is yours."

"Yours?" Aiden asks. "You mean ours."

Coach sighs and runs his hand over his nonexistent hair. "No, boys, I meant yours. It'll be announced after the Cup is won, but I won't be coaching next year. I'm going to retire."

"Retire? Why?" Maksim asks.

"I want to see my grandkids play sports, rekindle my

relationship with my wife after traveling through most of our marriage. She'll probably want to kill me after a month. It's been a fun ride, boys, and I had hopes we'd win a championship this year to make it all that much sweeter, but I can't keep waiting for the Cup to come back here. I gave my notice to Gerhardt this afternoon."

"Fuck," Ford says and hangs his head.

"No tears, boys. I'll see you out there."

We file out into the hallway, and since Aiden is the captain, he gets everyone pumped up.

"We do this for Coach!" he yells, and everyone cheers.

We each skate out, and I only glance up once. Trevor is up there and shaking his head at me as if he's trying to tell me something. York looks happy as shit for some reason, and Ande looks on the verge of tears. If I had to guess, I'd say the guys were right, they're sisters.

Fuck.

But how could I not have known I slept with sisters? I rack my brain for what I know about York and not one detail surfaces. God, I really was a shallow bastard.

After the game, which we won, I'm eager to get out of the locker room because not knowing feels like slowly draining all my blood instead of just severing the artery and bleeding out fast. But when I leave the locker room, they aren't there. Instead, the only woman I know who is waiting is Tedi. And fuck that girl can keep a secret.

"Hey, who's the woman with Ande?"

She stares at me. "What about her?"

"Who is she?"

She shrugs. "I don't know. But Ande and everyone else is already at Carmelo's."

"What? Why?" Ford says. "I told Lena no Carmelo's tonight. We have to get home with Annabelle and—"

"Your parents came and got Annabelle. It's just Lena there," Tedi tells Ford.

His forehead wrinkles. "Why?"

"You'll find out," she says. I don't miss the way she glances at me when she says it.

"Tedi, what do you know? Tell me?" I beg.

"Sorry. I've been sworn to secrecy. But I'm going to be honest, tie up those laces and get ready because you have a problem on your hands." She walks with Tweetie to his car.

I groan as I head to mine. There's no message on my phone from Ande and I really wish there were. I guess Carmelo's is where this showdown will happen. I haven't felt this nervous since my first game in the league.

After I park, I open the door, loosening my tie because I'm already anxious and sweating. Ande gives me a half wave when I enter the bar. She's sitting in a circular booth, and I walk over, not seeing York until it's too late.

"Hey, Cory," York says first.

"Hey." I look at Ande. "Do you know who this is?" I point at York.

"She's only known me her entire life," York answers for her, and it pisses me off for some reason.

I shift in place. "So..." I want to ask, but at the same time I don't want to know.

"We're sisters, Cory," Ande says quietly, and I take the seat beside her. "And I—"

"It's funny, remember how I came out here a few months ago? After we hooked up in Denver all those times you came through town?"

I say nothing but feel my jaw clench. My life is going to implode right now and it's all my own doing. All I want to do is go back to bed and share a night like the one I had with Ande last night.

"Well, I came to Florida to see my sister, and imagine my surprise when I find out that a certain hockey player from the Fury has been chasing after her?" York's expression is smug.

I glance over my shoulder and see all the guys at another table with their other halves, being filled in. All their faces are filled with sympathy.

"It was a long time ago," I tell Ande. "Not since we got back together."

Ande opens her mouth to speak, but York cuts her off again. York is clearly enjoying this a lot more than Ande.

"So we came up with a little plan." York smiles and there's nothing genuine about it.

"York," Ande says and looks at me with tears in her eyes. "I'm sorry, Cory. When it started, I was so mad that you'd slept with my sister, but—"

"To make you fall in love with Ande, make you think she was falling for you, and she'd cut you off, break your heart like you've done to so many other women."

York's words slice me in pieces. Tears flow from Ande's eyes now.

Ande slides closer to me. "Please listen to me." She puts her hand over mine. "I forgive you now. I should've never agreed to such a stupid plan because I think I knew I'd fall in love with you, and I have, Cory. So much, with my entire heart."

I slide my hand out from hers. "You orchestrated this whole thing? To hurt me?" I stand and step back from the booth.

"That was before. But I forgive you. I mean, we weren't

even a couple when you slept with her. I've wanted to tell you for a long time."

I shake my head to get my brain to work. "But you didn't tell me."

"Because I was enjoying being with you. Because I was falling in love with you." She follows me out of the booth while York remains seated.

"And what exactly do you forgive me for?" My voice is void of emotion. I can't believe Ande did this to me.

"For sleeping with York that weekend when you'd been chasing me and telling me you wanted to be with me. It made me think you were playing me. That I was just a conquest or a good time for you to have when you were in Florida and then you'd have different girls everywhere you traveled. But I see that's not true now. And I do trust you." She reaches for me again, but I back up out of reach.

I mull over everything she just said and frown when something stands out. "I didn't sleep with York that weekend she came to visit you." My gaze cuts to York, who has a self-satisfied smile on her face. "She reached out to see if I wanted to hook up with her, but I ended it as soon as I heard from her."

"What?" Ande's mouth hangs open for a second and she glances over her shoulder at her sister. "York?"

She shrugs. "I had to get you to see the guy for who he is, Ande. Sure, he ended it with me, but you'd only be his flavor of the month for so long. Eventually he'd find someone else."

Ande's shoulders sag and fresh tears stream down her face. "How could you lie? I told you how I felt about him."

York slides out of the booth. "Because you deserve better than some hockey player who sticks his dick in a different woman in every state."

"Are you sure it wasn't because you couldn't have me, but Ande could?" My voice is laced with venom because the picture is crystal fucking clear to me.

"Don't we have a high opinion of ourselves?" She puts her arm around Ande. "Let's go, sis."

Ande shrugs out of her hold. "Can we talk?" she asks me. "Let me explain the whole thing. You're only getting bits and pieces."

I shake my head. My chest feels as if it's caving in. "I was truthful with you, Ande. Always. We're over."

I shove my hands into my pockets and walk to the back of the bar to get some space from everyone. I really want to scream and hit something, but I won't do that in front of her.

I hear Trevor talking to her. I didn't even realize he was here. "Let's get you home, honey. York, maybe some space right now. Surely there's a hotel you can stay at."

"She's my sister."

"Then act more sisterly," Trevor snipes.

When I turn around a minute later, Ande is gone. That's when I storm out back and hit a trash can, tearing up my knuckles and making them bloody, just like my heart.

CHAPTER 28

Ande

Trevor escorts me out of Carmelo's, a place I'd be happy to never step foot in again. He gets me in his car, and we drive back to my house. He's in the middle of making me tea when the doorbell rings.

I rush to the door, hoping it's Cory—maybe when he thought it over, he realized we could talk this out—but it's York.

"I don't want to see you. You lied to me," I say through the door.

"Ande, I did it for your own good. Look, you're hurt."

I open the door, standing in the doorway. "I wouldn't be if you would've stayed out of it. Or how about been honest from the beginning by telling me he turned you down that night? Sure, it would've been uncomfortable, but at least I would've given him an honest chance. It's like you have some problem with me being happy."

I go to shut the door, but she stops me, and she must have a personal trainer these days because I'm no match for her. "Let's see, you were Dad's favorite. Always got his attention with those book nights you guys had. And you'd make jokes like I wouldn't understand. Then he died and he leaves you the executor of the will. If I wanted something, I had to go through you."

"He did it because you'd already left home. You weren't there when he died. I stayed. I stood by his side, held his hand as he took his last breath. And I did that alone. All by myself because you couldn't be bothered. If I remember correctly, you had a vacation booked that you would've lost money on."

She sits on my chair and Trevor brings over two cups of tea.

"Can I get a shot in it?" she asks Trevor.

"Be happy I gave you tea at all," he says and disappears —probably somewhere he can eavesdrop.

"Another guy you have wrapped around your finger." She rolls her eyes.

"Should I apologize for having a good friend? For forming friendships and relationships with other people? I always thought you didn't want that." I sip my tea, happy that Trevor put an ice cube in it.

"We're just different."

"Yeah, we are, which is why I should've never agreed to this scam." I'd do anything to go back and not have to see the hurt I caused in Cory's eyes.

She slumps back in her chair. "I went to Dad's funeral. I just hid behind a tree. I didn't want you to see me."

"York," I sigh. "Why?"

She shrugs. "I'm messed up. I didn't want to hear how I should've been there when he was sick. I didn't want to feel... anything."

"And you think I did? That I wanted the loneliness and heartbreak? To know that I was pretty much alone in this world?"

"You always had Brit and Sophie. Now you have all these people here. You attach strings to everyone you meet, whereas I cut them. We're just different."

I nod because that's the truth.

"I'm sorry," she says. "At first, I just told you I'd hooked up with someone that night because I was embarrassed and didn't want to admit that he'd rejected me. I didn't know about our Cory connection, and I didn't think it would make a difference one way or the other. Who cares if it was a lie so I could save face? Then after I found out that Cory had been pursuing you, I rationalized it by telling myself I was saving you from getting hurt, but I think maybe Cory was right and I felt like he was yet another person picking you over me."

I'm so pissed at my sister, but it still hurts to hear that she feels this way about herself.

"Then be a kinder person," Trevor says from wherever he's listening.

"Trevor," I say.

"He's right. When you told me how much Cory was chasing you, I was so jealous. I let that cloud my thinking. Cory didn't care about me. I was always the one checking his schedule and messaging him to hook up. He never stayed behind, and I never wanted him to. Or maybe I did. I don't know. But the fact that he wanted more with you pissed me off."

"God, York..." I don't know what to say beyond that because she sounds like pure evil. I can't believe we were raised by the same dad.

She crosses her legs on the chair and holds the teacup in both hands. "I'm really sorry, Ande. I should've been more sisterly—and kinder, as someone put it." She chuckles, but I don't.

"You can't sabotage my life like that."

"I know." She frowns and nods.

"I mean it. I just lost the first man I really loved. How I

feel for him isn't even close to how I felt for Michael. Now he thinks I'm the worst human being ever."

"Want me to call him and try to fix it?" she offers.

"No!" Trevor yells.

I shake my head. "We'll see what happens. Maybe after he cools off, he'll actually talk to me, but if he doesn't, I have to live with that. It's my own fault."

"Just remember, he was still screwing around until right before you guys got together. The blogs reported it. It's not like you made his reputation out of thin air. He has reason to be sorry too."

I smile softly, not sure we're on the same page. "Have you ever thought about therapy?"

She scoffs. "That's the worst part—I'm in therapy. But I'm not very honest with my therapist. Maybe I should change that."

I laugh for the first time tonight. "You think?"

She puts her teacup on the table. "I want to get out of here in case Cory comes over to talk." She stands and opens her arms. "I do love you even if I don't show it."

I set my teacup next to hers and stand to hug her. "I love you too, Pattie."

She smacks my back. "You know I hate that nickname."

"Which is why I get to call you it to your face for the next year without any repercussions from you. Payback for fucking with my life."

She nods and draws back, never one for physical intimacy. "Fine. See you around, Candy Ande."

We go to my front door, and she opens it, walks through, stops one more time before she turns the corner, then walks away.

I shut the door and sit back on the couch. "You can come out, Trevor."

"No offense, but I can't believe you two are related." He busies himself in the kitchen.

"What are you doing?"

"Just getting everything ready. Don't get all excited when the doorbell rings. It's Gregg delivering the heartbreak goods."

"Heartbreak goods?" I ask.

"Everything we need to fast-track this heartbreak of yours."

Just then the doorbell rings and Trevor answers the door.

"Oh, sweetie." Gregg hands Trevor the bag and pulls me into his arms. "Trev told me everything. It's okay, cry it out." He holds me tightly and taps my back in a rhythm. Rub, rub, tap, tap. Rub, rub, tap, tap.

"Gregg," I say after a minute.

"Yeah, sweetie?" he answers as he rocks me.

"I'm feeling sick."

He releases me at once. "Sorry, I tend to get a little mommy when my friends hurt."

"No, thank you."

They don't let me have one drop of alcohol. Instead, they have me eat pizza, cake, and ice cream with orange soda, which they say cures all. We play games, watch movies, and at some point, all three of us fall asleep in my bed.

When I wake up with the two of them on either side of me, I check my phone, but nothing from Cory. I really ruined it for myself. He's obviously not coming to talk since it's now three in the morning.

I look up the hockey blog that Jana loves, and there I am a crying mess, Trevor holding me up as we exit Carmelo's. With captions like, "the it couple is broken," "rumor is

Cory's already at the tattoo removal place," and "Ande crushed when Cory gives her the cold shoulder."

There's a lot that's untrue. No one has the sister twist, which surprises me. The gang must have kept tight lipped on that, which just further proves what good people they all are.

It was just last night that we made love. A night I never wanted to end. Now we're over, all because I was too afraid to be honest with him when I expected that in return. No wonder he's done with me. I'd be done with me too.

"Just get some sleep, sweetie." Gregg takes my hand and turns toward me. "We're here for you."

"Thank you," I say to both of them although only Gregg hears it. He squeezes my hand while Trevor snores in my other ear.

I'm not sure I could ever leave Florida because of my friendship with Trevor and Gregg, but getting away from Cory and not worrying about running into him sounds pretty good right now. Every time I saw him—whether at a restaurant, at the beach, or on TV—would be like picking a scab and allowing it to bleed. Yeah, no thank you. Maybe running away is my best option.

CHAPTER 29

Cory

I wake up with a skull-pounding headache and a dry mouth.

"Morning, sunshine." Kane is sitting in a chair next to my bed with his feet up on the mattress and a coffee in his hands.

"Why are you in my apartment?"

"At first I was worried about you hurting yourself or breaking all your furniture, then I worried about you dying in your own pile of vomit because you drank half of Carmelo's bar last night." He drops his feet to the floor and stands. "Come have breakfast."

I lift the sheets. "I'm not hungry. How did I get in my boxers?" I follow him, snagging some sweatpants off the floor to put on.

"Well, lucky for you we share a locker room, so I've seen your shit plenty. But you thought I was Ande for a while. Let me tell you that was an experience."

"What? You're fucking around, right?" I follow him, squinting with every step because my brain feels like Jell-O.

"Afraid not." He dishes out some eggs, toast, and hash browns he obviously made while I was asleep. "I already ate, so this is all to help you get over your damn hangover."

"Shit, man, I'm sorry."

He shrugs and sits on the stool across from me, handing me a fork. "It's okay. But more important, how are you feeling this morning?"

I run through last night in my head for a second. Ande and York. York and Ande. Sisters. "Fuck. They're sisters. That's all I can think of."

"Yeah, it's fucked up, but other than that, anything else you want to do right now?"

I look up at him, confused. "No."

"Nothing at all?"

I fork a piece of egg and bring it to my mouth. "You make a mean breakfast."

"You should try my French toast and peameal bacon. I'm a forever bachelor. You learn to cook after a while." He sips his coffee.

"Pea what?" I stop eating and look at him.

Kane rolls his eyes. "Canadian bacon to you yanks. Anyway, stop changing the subject."

I sigh. "I feel like you're looking for something else from me?"

He shakes his head. "What are you gonna do about Ande, asshole?"

"Nothing. She played me. She purposely wanted to break me, and she did. I loved her, man."

"I know. You tattooed her name on your chest."

I point the fork at him. "Exactly!"

"But you also slept with her sister. And her sister lied to her and told her that she'd slept with you after you were already pursuing Ande."

"And?"

"And that'll fuck with someone who has trust issues. Seriously, man, I know you were brought up by Ward and June Cleaver."

"Who?"

He shakes his head. "This damn generation. The Cleavers?"

I shake my head and shrug, not knowing who he's talking about.

"You had a great childhood with parents who loved you and all that shit, right?"

I nod.

"From what I hear, Ande had a mom who deserted her and a dad who ended up addicted to pills and died. An estranged sister, an ass of an ex-boyfriend who cheated on her. She's not exactly used to people sticking around for her."

I bury my head in my plate. Ande told me all that. She was worried about dating me because of her insecurities, but they all seemed to vanish once we'd been dating for a while.

"She purposely set out to hurt me." I fight the reason I cannot go to her now.

"In the end, she fell in love with you."

"It was all an act," I say.

"No, it wasn't. Do you remember how she looked at you? Surely you know in your heart how much that girl loves you. Don't be ignorant. At the end of the day, you can do whatever you want, but you need to look at the whole situation before you decide, not just cherry-pick the parts you want." Kane's getting angry, and I lean back, wondering why he cares so much. "Listen Cory"—when he uses my first name, he sounds so much like a dad—"some of us come from shitty childhoods, and shitty childhoods can fuck a person up."

"I know."

"Some people deserve a second chance to get it right.

She gave you one."

I say nothing, so he continues.

"You need to really think it over before you decide to walk away from what you two might have."

He makes his point just as my doorbell rings. He stands and answers the door. I know who it is before they even emerge from the hallway, because I can hear their voices.

"Why are you guys here?" I ask, watching my parents walk into my kitchen.

"Because I swore I'd never let you make a mistake without telling you first." My mom comes up to me and hugs me. "Go put a shirt on."

I stand and my dad hugs me too. "Son." He nods at me when I pull away.

I go into my bedroom and pull a T-shirt out of my drawer while I hear my mom asking Kane how he prepares such fluffy eggs and telling him that the hash browns could be a tad crispier and how she uses butter and oil to get that effect. I hurry out of my room before I put my T-shirt on to try to save Kane.

"Why are you guys here again?" I step back into the kitchen. It's not that I don't want to see my parents. It's just that I think I've already had more lecturing than I can handle hungover.

"Oh look, Cindy, there's the tattoo," my dad says, pointing at my chest.

"Let me see my future daughter-in-law's handwriting." My mom comes over and inspects the ink.

"It's still healing," I say, backing away from her touch. "And I'm assuming you're here because of the stupid blog, so you know she's not your future daughter-in-law." I pull my T-shirt over my head.

"Oh no, she is." Mom goes back into my kitchen. "Want

some chocolate chip pancakes like old times?" My mom doesn't wait for my answer before she digs into my cabinets, searching for what she needs. "This is pitiful, you have nothing."

"I can run to the store while you talk to Beaver here. What do you need?" Kane asks, and my parents crack up.

"Oh, we're no Ward and June," my dad says with humor.

My mom takes a receipt from the counter and writes down the ingredients she needs. "Thanks, Kane, I really appreciate it."

"No problem. I'll be back soon. Maybe you can talk some sense into him."

Kane leaves after I flip him off behind my parents' backs.

"Come sit." My parents take me to the family room, sandwiching me between them like when I was ten and in trouble. "This girl, Ande? You love her?"

"I did until she deceived me."

"Tell us what happened. How do you go from tattooing her name on your skin to breaking up?" my dad asks.

I know they're not leaving without hearing it all, so I tell them the whole story up until last night, when everything came to a head. Of course, I leave out the details about us sleeping together or her spectacular blow job skills, but they get the gist.

"She wanted to hurt you," Dad says, looking at my mom.

I nod. "Yes."

"But she never did because she fell in love with you, then she wanted to tell you but was afraid she'd lose you because she's lost everyone she's ever loved before?" Mom says like she understands Ande or something.

"I mean, I guess you could say that, but yeah, she set out to hurt me. You don't do that to someone you love."

"She didn't love you when she set out to do that," my dad

says. "In fact, she didn't like you much at all, son, and I can't say I blame her."

I stew on that for a moment before I open my mouth and say something disrespectful. "Regardless, what type of person does that make her?"

How can I be the only one who gets this?

My mom taps my leg with her hand. "We never told you this because we didn't want you to think differently of your grandparents, but when I first brought your dad home, Grandma and Grandpa weren't happy."

I look from my mom to my dad and back. "Why?"

My dad laughs. "Because I'm Black," he answers as though it's obvious.

"They were so close-minded and didn't think I could really love your father. They thought he was dating me as some prize to show off or something stupid like that. But I told them I loved your father, and I was going to date him no matter what they thought of it. Gradually, they got better, but for a while there, I thought I might have to step away from them. If they couldn't accept your father, I couldn't have them as part of my life. I wanted the love we shared to be celebrated, not chastised." She looks at my dad.

"Could you imagine if we didn't agree with a decision you were making in your life and you walked away from us? Now you're alone in the world. How would you feel?" my dad asks. "Sure, your mom had me, but what if something had happened to me? She would've already walked away from her parents and family. How would you feel if you didn't have us, Cory?"

I shrug. "It would suck."

I think of holidays and the traditions that are still a part of my life. The fact that I can call my parents for anything at any time and I know I'll take priority. The fact that they're here right now after seeing that I broke up with Ande. I know I'm lucky.

My mom blinks back tears. "Good people make bad decisions, Cory. You've made plenty."

"Technically, you wouldn't be in this predicament if you hadn't decided to sleep with someone in every town," my dad says.

I huff. "It wasn't every town."

"Well... that's up for debate, but you're not completely innocent here," he says.

"You don't have a brother, but what if your cousin Malcolm would've slept with Ande at some point? How would you feel?"

"I'd be pissed." My answer is quick and truthful.

"Fortunately, you can't put yourself in Ande's shoes. You grew up with great parents who love and adore you. You've never been abandoned. Even Grandma and Grandpa came around before we married. But try to be understanding. In the end, she fell in love with you, and it sounds like she wanted to do what was right." My mom pats my leg and stands because the door opens and Kane comes in.

I look at my dad. "What if?"

He smiles, clearly knowing where my mind is. What if I fall in love and she breaks my heart?

"Maybe you're understanding her fear a little more than you think. Love is putting all your trust and faith in someone else. And when you love someone, sometimes forgiveness is the greatest gift you can give them. It's always a risk though. What you have to figure out is if it's worth it. Is Ande worth the risk?" He pats my back and stands.

I stay on the couch while Kane takes lessons on pancakes from my mom and my dad finishes my breakfast, complimenting Kane on his fluffy eggs. Instead of waiting for more food, I grab my keys and wallet from the table and start walking toward the door.

My mom holds out her arm like she used to when she had to slam on the brakes in the car. "Go shower. No woman wants a man reeking of alcohol to come groveling at her doorstep."

I circle back around and shut my bedroom door to take the fastest shower of my life because I have my answer. Ande *is* worth the risk.

CHAPTER 30

"My navigational skills got me to you."
—Cory

Ande

I wake up to my shower running.

"What the hell?" I groan at Trevor nudging me awake.

"We had our night of sulking. Now it's time to pick ourselves up," he says.

I roll over, pulling the comforter over my head. "Go away. I'm staying here all day."

"We don't lie in bed and feel sorry for ourselves all day. Come on." He throws the covers off. "Don't make me undress you and dump a bucket of cold water on you. Or worse, have Gregg give you a sponge bath."

I spring up. "I'm up."

Gregg laughs and escorts me into the bathroom, shutting the door once I'm inside the steamy room.

My shoulders fall for a moment, remembering the night before, but I undress and step into the scalding water. Damn, it's so fucking hot, it's all I can do to get to the handle to lower the temperature.

I shampoo and condition my hair, and I even shave because I don't want to leave this room. Trevor and Gregg are going to force me to do things I don't want to do. Probably a brunch or something where I'll have to make conversation.

But a knock on the door says I can't hide anymore, so I turn off the water, wrap my hair in a towel, and dry off my body.

Another knock.

"I'm applying body lotion. Give me a break!" I shout, pumping lotion into my hand and spreading it over my arms and legs.

"Hurry!" Trevor yells and I make a face at the door. "Don't look at me like that. Just get out here."

I shake my head and put on my facial moisturizer. I shake out and towel dry my hair, having no energy to style it. When I finally emerge, I go to my closet to pick out clothes for the day. I decide on cutoff shorts and a T-shirt. In my hamper is Cory's Florida Fury jersey, so I pick it up and take it into the living area where Trevor and Gregg are.

"Do either one of you want this? Or I can just take the kitchen shears to it." I look up and Trevor and Gregg aren't there, but Cory is. He's got dark circles under his eyes, but he's showered and clean. I look around. "What are you doing here?"

"I'd hate to see you take kitchen shears to it, but I'd understand if you did."

I drop the jersey on the breakfast stool and head into the kitchen. Mostly because I need to stay busy.

"Why are you here?" Everything in me wants to hope, but I push back the instinct.

"Because I love you," he says plainly. "I should've stopped to get you flowers or candies or whatever guys do to say they're sorry, but I just wanted to get here as soon as I could. My mom made me shower, and that delayed me a bit and—"

I laugh at the idea of his mom making him shower.

He gets up from the chair and meets me on the other

side of the breakfast bar. "I'm sorry for how I acted. I was taken by surprise, but I should've listened to your explanation."

I pour myself a coffee and lift a cup for him.

"Not yet," he says.

"I'm not sure I had a good explanation. I should never have done what I did."

"Do you regret it?" he asks, stopping me before I can leave the kitchen.

I look up into his eyes. "Of course I do. More than anything. I was just so angry, but that was only because York told me you'd slept with her that night she came into town. I didn't know you'd actually ended it with her."

"I'm glad you did it."

I can't help but laugh. "You've lost your mind. You're happy that I tricked you into falling in love with me?"

He takes my hand and leads me to the couch. "How did you trick me?"

"I set out to make you fall in love with me so I could hurt you."

"Sure, you wanted me to fall in love with you, but you didn't drug me or anything. I fell in love with you because you're who you are. And you didn't want to hurt me. You were going to tell me. Looking back, I can actually see all the times I think you might have been trying to get it out."

"You're reaching for reasons to rationalize what I did, Cory."

He shakes his head. "I just need an answer to one question."

"I really am on the pill. I wouldn't trick you and get pregnant."

"No." He laughs. "That wasn't the question."

"Then what is?" I bite my lower lip, waiting.

"Do you love me?"

My shoulders drop. "You know I do."

"But say it," he insists, taking my hands.

"I love you, Cory."

"That's all I need. I want us to forget all the other bull-shit, because I love you too. I want us to start fresh from this point on." His one hand releases mine and comes up to cradle my cheek. "I love you so much, Ande, I never want to be without you. God, I barely made it twelve hours."

I place my hand over his on my face. "Are you sure? What changed your mind?"

"Someone made me realize that I failed you last night. So, I just want you to know from this day forward, I will never abandon you. I will never leave you. I will stay and I will listen when we face a challenge, I promise."

Tears well up in my eyes and I shake my head. "You shouldn't be apologizing. I'm the one to blame, not you."

"Let's just start over, like I said." He holds out his hand. "I'm Cory. Cory Freeman."

"I'm Ande, like the candy."

"No, you're beautiful."

I inhale at what now seems to be his nickname for me. "I don't usually sleep around on the first date, but..." I stand and hold my hand for him.

He places his hand in mine. "First, I want you to meet my parents."

My mouth drops open. "You do?"

"They should probably meet their future daughter-in-law."

"Cory," I whisper.

He takes me in his arms as I bury my face in his chest. "What is it?"

I stare up at him with my chin on his chest. "I just can't believe we got here."

"I can. I knew the minute you sat next to me on that bus that you were going to be mine one way or another."

"You with your lack of navigational skills?" I ask, lightly pushing his stomach, but his arms tighten around me.

"My navigational skills got me to you."

"Very true." I rise on my tiptoes. "I love you."

"I'll never tire of hearing you say that." He bends down farther and kisses me softly before he suddenly tears his lips away from me. "York? Is that after Peppermint Pattie?"

I nod, and he laughs.

"You don't want to carry on that tradition, do you?"

I pretend to pout. "I already have my kids' names picked out. Godiva, Dulce, and Cherry. We could throw in a Tootsie if we have a fourth."

"No Cory Jr.?"

I laugh and pull him back down to my lips. "Kiss me again."

"Anytime."

And he does kiss me all the way to the bedroom. We can squeeze in a quickie before meeting the folks.

EPILOGUE

"Take a look at the future of Florida Fury."
—M. Gerhardt

Cory

We're all attending Coach Vittner's retirement party in the off-season. Things have been amazing between Ande and me and I'm enjoying my time off, but I'd be lying if I said I wasn't looking forward to getting back on the ice. Coach's replacement hasn't been named yet, but since the season doesn't start for a while, there isn't a huge rush.

Ande and I find the table that's assigned to us before we mingle. She hugs the women and I shake the guys' hands. The women talk about where they got their dresses and show each other their shoes. They don't see each other as much since we're not playing right now. A lot of players use the time off to travel and visit family, vacation, or just lie low. To be honest, Ande and I have been lost in our own bubble. With all my time off, I'm at the office more than Trevor would like. The gleam and bragging rights of knowing professional hockey players have worn off in Trevor's world.

I'm chatting with some of the guys when I catch Ande's eyes, and I know we're on the same page. Dinner and dessert, one dance, and we sneak out. For now, I'm biding my time.

Imogen is really showing now, and every woman touches her stomach. I'm hoping it's not contagious because

I want to do this right without scaring Ande. I have a ring, but I want to propose when she doesn't expect it. First, I want her to move in with me, but she's very attached to her apartment. Something about plants and light.

My parents adore her, and she actually talks to my mom once a week. About what? I have no fucking clue, but I can't deny that I love it. And I think Ande enjoys having a motherly presence in her life too.

"Can everyone please be seated?" someone says over a microphone.

I go over to Ande and guide her to our table, pulling the chair out for her.

"Thank you." She grins up at me.

When I fold myself into the seat next to her, she places her hand on my thigh as though it's second nature. Our relationship is everything I've ever wanted. The ease with which we coexist together is once in a lifetime as far as I'm concerned. I kiss her whenever I want, and she likes to cuddle and watch television at night. She steals my popcorn, but that's okay. I'll share anything with her. I just love her so fucking much.

Mr. Gerhardt goes up and gives a speech about what a great guy Coach Vittner is, how much he'll be missed, and how whoever fills his shoes has their work cut out for them. We all clap, and the waitstaff comes out to serve dinner.

After he gets off the stage, Mr. Gerhardt comes over to our table and greets us. "Excuse me, Kane, can I have a word?"

Kane still hasn't officially decided whether he's going to play next year. There are rumors that if he doesn't retire, Mr. Gerhardt is going to trade him. As he and Mr. Gerhardt walk off, we all look at one another, hoping that doesn't happen.

We eat our salads and soups. Kane returns a short time

later with no readable expression on his face, because that's Kane for you.

Tweetie teeters on the back legs of his chair at the table next to ours. "What did he want?"

Kane shrugs. "Nothing. Just something about Coach."

"Shit, I thought maybe he was gonna tell you a trade went through or some crap." Tweetie lowers the chair back down and goes back to his table's discussion, probably filling them in on Kane's news.

I look across the table and study Kane for a second. He looks stressed. There's a little bit of sweat on his forehead and he keeps drinking his water.

I eat some more of my meal, then I can't resist leaning in to whisper into Ande's ear, "I want you naked."

"You always want that," she says in a regular tone, drawing attention from my teammates.

"Stop dirty talking your girl," Warner says. "But I have to tell you all, month five is pretty fucking fantastic for the libido. Gen can't get enough."

Imogen hits him hard on the shoulder. "Warner!"

"Did you forget we're not in the locker room?" Maksim asks.

"You talk about us in the locker room?" Paisley asks, her mouth hanging open.

"No, Kotik. No. Not me."

We all roll our eyes at Maksim. He's not the biggest talker, but we all have our moments.

"I was just telling them the perks of pregnancy. You know, in case any of them are considering." Warner looks at Imogen as though he's innocent.

She shakes her head and eats. After a minute, she says, "Want to know a perk, ladies? You can eat whatever you want." She stabs a piece of Warner's steak and brings it over onto her plate and cuts into it.

He wisely shuts up.

"Are we going to turn into that?" Ande whispers to me.

"I hope so," I say.

She smiles at me.

Dinner ends and the dancing starts. I'm ready to hightail it out of here, but Ande has second thoughts. While we're slow dancing and I'm showing her my moves, she tells me we should stay, that it would be rude if we left this early.

"Ugh, fine."

She giggles and my hand slides down her back to her ass, which I squeeze.

"Cory," she says.

"I love your ass and you love when I squeeze it, which brings up a question."

She draws back and looks up at me. "No butt implants."

"Nah, your ass is perfect. But I really want that amazing ass on my couch and in my bed every damn day and night."

"It practically is."

I shake my head. "You know what I'm asking, beautiful."

"Then ask it straight, Cory."

"Move in with me. I don't care if it's your place or mine. If you like the light better at yours, whatever, or we can get something we pick out together. Whatever you want as long as you're in my bed every night and every morning when I wake up."

"Well... I suppose so." She laughs.

My lips descend on hers, stripping the laughter from her. I slip my tongue past her lips and things get hot and heavy, so I take her hand and tug her toward the hallway.

"What are we doing?"

"I want you alone for, like, five minutes." I try to open a

door in the hallway, but it's locked. I know the bathrooms aren't private with this many people around.

"We can wait to celebrate when we get home," she says.

"You might be able to, but I think I feel like Imogen does."

She laughs as I lead her farther down the hall and open an unlabeled door, hoping like hell it's a closet door.

When I flick on the light, I shout, "Holy shit!"

"You said you locked it!" Jana screams and smacks Kane on the chest. His hand is up the slit in her dress and her lipstick is smudged across his face. She's sporting a mess of just-fucked hair.

"Shit, so you two are really..." My mouth hangs open.

"Excuse us." Ande reaches past me for the door handle. "Carry on."

She shuts the door, but I'm still frozen to the spot.

"Come, Cory." She tugs on my arm.

Damn, the rumors were true. Hell, I can't believe Kane didn't tell me.

"Let me find somewhere else," I say to Ande, but she's shaking her head.

"I don't want to ruin anyone else's secrets. We're going to have cake. We can wait until we get home. I'm sure the cake is just as good." She stops at the cake table once we're back in the party room.

"Are you comparing my dick to cake?"

"No, it's just cake is really good, babe."

I narrow my eyes at her. "Maybe if it's covering my dick."

"Can you please stop saying dick?" She smiles at the elderly couple passing us. "Here. Try some. Super yummy." She hands the woman a piece of cake as though she's been hired to pass it out.

"I'm fully insulted and so is my dick. You have a lot of kissing up to do when we get home."

She rolls her eyes and we both laugh. The clinking of a glass interrupts us, and we move to where we can see the podium.

Mr. Gerhardt stands there. "Hey, everyone, gather round. I have an announcement to make."

Kane comes out of the hallway and goes back to his seat, picking up his glass, while Jana slides in from the other direction and sits at her family table.

"When I bought the Florida Fury, I had hopes it would be where it is today. We're popular with our fans, and we've managed to grow the popularity of the game in a Southern state. We've built a solid foundation for our team, and now we just need to win that Cup. We've had a lot of growth these past few years, so I'm excited to announce our new coach who I think can build on what Coach Vittner put together and hopefully take us all the way there. He was a player himself and although this will be his first year of coaching..."

My head whips in Kane's direction, and he looks at me from the corner of his eye.

Shit, he did retire?

"Kane Burrows has happily accepted the coaching position. He'll be announcing his retirement from the league in a press conference tomorrow. Please welcome him in his new role in the Florida Fury organization."

The applause starts hesitantly, but it picks up as Kane walks up to the podium and shakes Mr. Gerhardt's hand. He raises his hand but says nothing. Maybe because Mr. Gerhardt didn't give him the microphone.

"Before I let you go, there's one more announcement I'd like to make. I'm tired and I'm old, guys," Mr. Gerhardt says.

A few people laugh. "So I'm really happy my gorgeous wife gave birth to an amazing daughter who is as smart as a whip and can probably take this team to places I could never imagine. Sometimes the old have to step out of the way of the young. Jana, come join me."

Jana looks around like a doe in headlights, but her mom hugs her as if she won an Academy Award. When Jana reaches the podium, Kane slides out of her way as though they're strangers and weren't just getting it on in the storage room.

"It's yours now, sweetheart. The Florida Fury is yours. Time for you to have the key to the owner's office."

Jana accepts the key her dad gives her but doesn't say anything as he kisses her cheek.

"Take a look at the future of Florida Fury." Mr. Gerhardt puts his hand out toward Jana and Kane, standing next to one another with forced smiles.

Shit. This will be interesting, to say the least.

The End

Cockamamie Unicorn Ramblings

After two deadline extensions and we finally finished Cory's book!

When we wrote Tropical Hat Trick it originally appeared in the Color Theory anthology. Cory and Ande's story was meant to be a short one involving a vacation fling. Then of course we got to thinking it would be a good intro into our Hockey Hotties series.

But because we wouldn't get our rights back in time, we decided we'd release Tropical Hat Trick in between books three and four. But because Ford's book led perfectly into Warner's we pushed Cory's book to be fifth in the series. Hence, we wanted to add in more of Warner and Imogen and Jana and Kane and you get where this all ended up.

This all meant we had to come up with a reason to why Ande and Cory wouldn't have kept in contact. Why Ande wouldn't be up for a relationship? Why would Cory have to fight for her? Because if you can't tell by now, we like it a lot when the hero has to pull out all the stops to get the woman he loves back. And boy did we have a lot of back and forth on this when we were plotting. Enter York. Not the most likeable character we've ever written, right? She did her job masterfully. We love writing about families but as we're sure some of you know, not all sibling relationships are healthy ones. And York and Ande's was a prime example of that.

Lucky for Ande she had Trevor who acted not only as a friend but filled a sort of brotherly role in her life. Add on a lot of fun scenes with him and some other drama profes-sional hockey players deal with, and you have their story.

Oh, and in case you're wondering. Those fan sites dissing and gossiping about all the women in professional athlete's lives really do exist. Sheesh.

Sometimes they don't come easy, and this was one that was a struggle for some reason or another. Hopefully in the end you loved their journey back to one another!

Other than that,
The entire Valentine PR group for everything!!!
Cassie from Joy Editing for line edits.
Ellie from My Brother's Editor for line edits.
Rosa from My Brother's Editor for proofreading.
Renita Lofton McKinney for being our go to diversity editor.
Hang Le for the cover and branding for the entire series. Those colors!
Regina Wamba for the photo of our Cory.
Bloggers who consistently carve out time to read, review and/or promote our work. Thank you for your continued support!
Piper Rayne Unicorns in our Facebook group who love our characters like as much as we do and provide us with a fun, interactive group! Thank you!
All the readers who took the time to read our story when there's so many choices out there. We're constantly amazed by your support and how much you stand behind our stories. It doesn't go unnoticed and we're truly grateful.

Next up is Kane and Jana. We've been teasing these two

for quite some time! Any guesses on what will happen now that they have to work side by side to make sure the Florida Fury win the cup?!?

xo,
Piper & Rayne

ABOUT PIPER & RAYNE

Piper Rayne is a USA Today Bestselling Author duo who write "heartwarming humor with a side of sizzle" about families, whether that be blood or found. They both have e-readers full of one-clickable books, they're married to husbands who drive them to drink, and they're both chauffeurs to their kids. Most of all, they love hot heroes and quirky heroines who make them laugh, and they hope you do, too!

ALSO BY PIPER RAYNE

Hockey Hotties

My Lucky #13

The Trouble with #9

Faking it with #41

Sneaking around with #34

Second Shot with #76

Offside with #55

Kingsmen Football Stars

You had your chance, Lee Burrows

You can't kiss the Nanny, Brady Banks

Over my Brother's Dead Body, Chase Andrews

The Baileys

Lessons from a One-Night Stand

Advice from a Jilted Bride

Birth of a Baby Daddy

Operation Bailey Wedding (Novella)

Falling for My Brother's Best Friend

Demise of a Self-Centered Playboy

Confessions of a Naughty Nanny

Operation Bailey Babies (Novella)

Secrets of the World's Worst Matchmaker

Winning My Best Friend's Girl

Rules for Dating your Ex

Operation Bailey Birthday (Novella)

The Greenes

My Beautiful Neighbor

My Almost Ex

My Vegas Groom

The Greene Family Summer Bash

My Sister's Flirty Friend

My Unexpected Surprise

My Famous Frenemy

The Greene Family Vacation

My Scorned Best Friend

My Fake Fiancé

My Brother's Forbidden Friend

The Modern Love World

Charmed by the Bartender

Hooked by the Boxer

Mad about the Banker

The Single Dad's Club

Real Deal

Dirty Talker

Sexy Beast

Hollywood Hearts

Mister Mom

Animal Attraction

Domestic Bliss

Bedroom Games

Cold as Ice

On Thin Ice

Break the Ice

Box Set

Charity Case

Manic Monday

Afternoon Delight

Happy Hour

Blue Collar Brothers

Flirting with Fire

Crushing on the Cop

Engaged to the EMT

White Collar Brothers

Sexy Filthy Boss

Dirty Flirty Enemy

Wild Steamy Hook-up

The Rooftop Crew

My Bestie's Ex

A Royal Mistake

The Rival Roomies

Our Star-Crossed Kiss

The Do-Over

A Co-Workers Crush